Cornelius Tacitus, Alfred John Church, William J. Brodribb

The Agricola of Tacitus

with a revised text, English notes, and map

Cornelius Tacitus, Alfred John Church, William J. Brodribb

The Agricola of Tacitus
with a revised text, English notes, and map

ISBN/EAN: 9783337405892

Printed in Europe, USA, Canada, Australia, Japan

Cover: Foto ©Andreas Hilbeck / pixelio.de

More available books at **www.hansebooks.com**

THE AGRICOLA OF TACITUS

WITH

A REVISED TEXT, ENGLISH NOTES, AND MAP.

BY

ALFRED J. CHURCH, M.A.

LINCOLN COLLEGE, OXFORD,

ONE OF THE ASSISTANT MASTERS IN MERCHANT TAYLORS' SCHOOL, LONDON

AND

W. J. BRODRIBB, M.A.

LATE FELLOW OF ST JOHN'S COLLEGE, CAMBRIDGE.

London:

MACMILLAN AND CO.

AND NEW YORK.

1894

Printed by C. J. CLAY, 1869.
Reprinted 1870, 1873, 1874, 1876, 1877, 1879,
1881, 1882, 1885, 1887,
1891, 1894.

PREFACE

THE Treatise on Germany and the Life of Agricola have, perhaps, been edited as frequently as any of the Latin Classics. They exhibit in a singularly convenient form the manner and genius of one of the greatest of ancient historians; and thus at once possess a great literary value, and are peculiarly useful as text-books in our Schools and Universities. About works which have been so diligently studied we can hardly expect to say much that is original. We have endeavoured, with the aid of recent editions, thoroughly to elucidate the text, explaining the various difficulties, critical and grammatical, which occur to the student. Information which is now amply supplied by the dictionaries of biography and geography we have thought it unnecessary to furnish. We have consulted throughout, besides the older commentators, the editions of Ritter and Orelli, but we are under special obligations to the labours of the recent German editors, Wex and Kritz, an obligation which must not be measured by the extent of our references to them.

We have followed, but with some important variations, the text of Orelli. A table is given of the passages in which we have adopted a different reading.

We frequently quote from our translation (published in 1868). It may be as well to explain that in some instances we have seen reason to modify the renderings there given.

A. J. C.
W. J. B.

London,
  January, 1869.

CONTENTS.

List of Editions and Translations of the Agricola and
Germania of Tacitus which have been consulted
by the present Editors. [This list is confined
to works of the present century.]

J. Aikin, 1823. Translation of the Agricola and Germania
with notes. 4th Edition. This is a work designed rather for
general readers than for scholars and students.

C. Roth, 1833. Edition of the Agricola, with learned and
copious German notes, which are however hardly adapted to ordinary students.

P. Frost, 1847. Edition of the Agricola and Germania, with
English notes. It is suitable for the use of schools, but is now
rather out of date.

Dr Latham, 1851. Edition of the Germania, for students of
philology and ethnology. Critical and grammatical difficulties
are not discussed.

F. C. Wex, 1852. Edition of the Agricola, with a thoroughly revised text, Prolegomena, in which every difficult and
corrupt passage is fully discussed, and Latin notes. This is the
most valuable of all recent editions of the Agricola, and is the
result of most laborious research.

F. C. Wex, 1852. Edition of the Agricola for the use of
Schools, without the Prolegomena and with the notes of the
larger edition translated into German.

M. Haupt, 1855. Edition of the Germania, with a new and
carefully revised text, for the use of Schools.

W. Smith, 1855. Edition of the Agricola and Germania,
with English notes, which are chiefly taken from Ruperti and
Passow, and with Boetticher's essay on the style of Tacitus.

A. J. Henrichsen, 1855. German translation of the Agricola
only partially complete.

W. S. Tyler, 1857. Edition of the Agricola and Germania,
with English notes, drawn from the best commentators, and
with a life of Tacitus. Published at New York. This is a useful edition, but the notes are rather too diffuse.

Kritz, 1859. Edition of the Agricola, mainly based upon
Wex, with Latin notes.

Kritz, 1860. Edition of the Germania, mainly based upon
Haupt, with Latin notes.

[Both these editions we have found very useful.]

K. A. Löw, 1862. German translation of the Germania, with
the Latin text, and notes.

N. Mösler, 1862. German translation of the Germania, with
the Latin text, and notes.

G. and F. Thudichum, 1862. German translation of the Germania, with the Latin text, and notes.

NOTES ON THE LIFE AND WRITINGS
OF TACITUS.

LITTLE or nothing is known of the life of Tacitus except what he tells us himself, or what we may gather from the Epistles of his friend, the younger Pliny. His *praenomen* is a matter of doubt. It is commonly written *Caius* (on the authority of Sidonius Apollinaris), but it is given as Publius in the best MS. of the *Annals*. The name *Cornelius* suggests a possible connection with the great patrician Gens which was thus designated. But there was also a plebeian house of the same name, and it must be remembered that in the time of the Empire the *nomina gentilia* had become widely diffused. With regard to his parentage we have at least a probable conjecture to guide us. The elder Pliny was, he tells us (*Nat. Hist.* VII. 17), acquainted with one Cornelius Tacitus, who was then a Procurator in Belgic Gaul, and who had a son. It has been supposed that this Tacitus was the historian's father. The similarity of name, the coincidence of dates, and the probability that at some time of his life our author was familiar with the neighbourhood of North-Eastern Gaul, incline us to accept the conjecture, which is further supported by the fact that the circumstances of his career seem to imply an origin which was respectable rather than dignified. A Procurator was generally a person of Equestrian rank. About the date of his birth nothing can be certainly affirmed. It is indeed approximately fixed by several expressions used by the younger Pliny. That writer says (*Epist.* VII. 20) that Tacitus and himself were "nearly equal in age

b

and rank (aetate et dignitate propemodum *aequales*)."
The question is how far *aequales* must be considered
to be modified by *propemodum*. We think the word
should be taken to imply a considerable difference.
Pliny himself says, "When I was a very young man
(*adolescentulus*) and you were at the height of your
fame and reputation, I earnestly desired to imitate
you." *Adolescentulus* is a very vague term, but Pliny
may be taken to define this application of it to himself
when he tells us (*Epist.* v. 8) that he was in his nine-
teenth year when he began to speak in the Forum.
He was, as he tells us himself (*Epist.* vi. 20), in his
eighteenth year when the famous eruption of Vesuvius
took place (A. D. 79), and he must therefore have been
born A.D. 61 or 62. We are inclined to put the
date of the birth of Tacitus at least ten years earlier.
In this conclusion we are supported by the passage
which we find in the third chapter of the *Life of
Agricola*. There he speaks of those who had survived
the evil days of Domitian as coming under two
classes, the young men who had become old, the old
'who had advanced to the very verge and end of
existence.' He must have included himself in the
former class. The *Agricola* was published before the
death of Nerva but after the adoption of Trajan, *i.e.*
in the latter part of the year 97. It may surprise us
that Tacitus could have spoken of himself as being
then an old man. But the term *senior* was technically
applied at Rome (Aul. Gellius, x. 28, quoting Tubero)
to those who had passed their forty-fifth year. And
C. Cotta (in a speech to the people preserved to us in
one of the fragments of Sallust) speaks of himself, he
being then forty-eight, as an old man. If Tacitus
was fifty in A.D. 97, he must have been born A.D. 47;

if an interval of fifteen years is thought too much
to be borne out by Pliny's *propemodum* (occurring,
it must be remembered, in a complimentary letter,
and from its very employment implying no incon-
siderable difference), we must not anyhow fix a later
date than A. D. 51 or 52.

The town of Interamna (now Terni) in Umbria
has been named as the birthplace of Tacitus. There
is no direct proof of the assertion, but it is known
that this town was in the third century the seat of
the family of the Emperor Tacitus. This prince, who
occupied the throne for a few months after the death
of Aurelian A.D. 275, was accustomed to claim descent
from the historian, and honoured his memory by directing that ten copies of his works should be annually
transcribed and placed in the public libraries.

If our conjecture as to the date of his birth be
correct, Tacitus must have attained the period of
youth in the great year (69) which witnessed the fall
of three Emperors. His descriptions of some of the
scenes of that time, among which we may specify the
entry of the Flavianist troops into Rome (*Hist.* III. 83),
look like the work of an eye-witness.

It has been suggested that Tacitus made the
acquaintance of Agricola at some time in the three
years (A. D. 74—77) during which that officer held the
government of Aquitania. There is, it has been
thought, a particularity about his description of
Agricola's administration which indicates the intimate
acquaintance of one who either held some official
position, or was otherwise closely connected with it.
This position may possibly have included something
of the intimate relation in which Agricola himself
at the opening of his career had stood to Suetonius

Paulinus (*Agr.* 5). However this may be, it is certain that at or before this time an intimate acquaintance had been formed between the two men. In A.D. 77 Agricola returned to Rome to fulfil the duties of the Consulship. During his year of office he betrothed his daughter (born A.D. 65) to his young friend. *Juveni mihi*, says Tacitus, *filiam despondit. Juvenis*, like other Latin terms denoting age, is elastic in its signification, but it is particularly applicable to one who was between his twenty-fifth and thirtieth year. The marriage was celebrated in the following year, the same in which Agricola assumed his command in Britain.

The illustrious alliance thus formed was probably the means of introducing Tacitus to a career of public distinction. His elevation, he says (*Hist.* I. 1) was "begun by Vespasian, augmented by Titus, and still further advanced by Domitian." What offices he may have held under the first and second of these princes, it is impossible to determine. Agricola himself was Quaestor and Tribune of the People before he reached the Praetorship. But the Quaestors were employed in the Provinces. If we suppose Tacitus to have remained at Rome we may conjecture that he filled the office of Aedile, and as Vespasian, his first patron died June 23, A.D. 79, that he was appointed to it early in that year. His next office was probably that of Tribune of the People, which, as Titus died Sept. 13, A.D. 81, he must have held either A. D. 80 or in the following year. We know from his own testimony (*Ann.* XI. 11) that he was Praetor A.D. 88, in which year Domitian celebrated the Ludi Saeculares. In 89 or 90 he left Rome with his wife, and did not return till after the death of Agricola, which took place

August 23, A.D. 93. (See *Agr.* ch. 45). It is certain, however, that he was in Rome during the last period of Domitian's reign. The language in which at the close of the *Agricola* he describes the horrors of that time is full of the bitterness, and even of the self-reproach of one who had been compelled to witness and to sanction by his presence the cruelties of the tyrant.

Domitian was assassinated Sept. 18, A. D. 95. Two years afterwards Tacitus was advanced to the dignity of the Consulship. Verginius Rufus had died in his year of office, and Tacitus was appointed to succeed him. He also delivered a funeral oration on his predecessor. " Hic supremus," says Pliny of Rufus (*Epist.* II. 1), " felicitati ejus cumulus accessit, laudator eloquentissimus."

In A. D. 100 he was appointed together with Pliny, who was then Consul elect, to conduct the impeachment preferred by the Province of Africa against their late Proconsul, Marcus Priscus. Pliny, who relates the trial at length (*Epist.* II. 11), describes his oratory by the epithet σεμνῶς. Here the public life of Tacitus terminated. We hear indeed in one of Pliny's letters (VI. 9) of his interesting himself in the candidature of one Julius Naso for some public office. We may gather from the letter that he was not then living at Rome, and, perhaps, as he was not aware that Naso had started under the auspices of Pliny, that he knew but little of what was going on in the capital.

The date of his death is not known, but that he at least lived down to the end of Trajan's reign, we may infer from *Ann.* II. 61, where he says that the Roman Empire " Nunc ad rubrum mare patescit," an expression which must refer to the successes obtained by Trajan in his Eastern expedition (A. D. 114—117).

The *Dialogus de Oratore*, which we have no hesitation in ascribing to the pen of Tacitus, was probably an early work. The expression which we find in ch. 1·7, "sextam jam felicis hujus principatus stationem qua Vespasianus rem publicam fovet," may not be intended to do more than fix the date of the imaginary conversation; but the passage indicates a more favourable opinion of the Emperor than he seems to have entertained in after years. (See *Hist.* II. 84, III. 34, &c.)

The *Agricola* was published towards the close of A. D. 97; the *Germany* in the following year. The *History* may with probability be ascribed to some year between A.D. 103 and 106. A very interesting letter of Pliny's (*Epist.* IX. 27) very probably refers to it. It was still, we know, in course of preparation when his *Epistles* VI. 16, 20 and VII. 33 were written. The first and second of these describe the famous eruption of Vesuvius, and were written at the historian's request. The third relates some particulars as to the prosecution of Baebius Massa in which Pliny had taken a part which he was anxious to have recorded. "Auguror," he writes, "historias tuas immortales futuras; quo magis illis (ingenue fatebor) inseri cupio." The publication of the *Annals* must be referred, as has before been said, to the close of Trajan's reign. Reference is made in *Ann.* XI. 11 to the *History* as an earlier work, "libris quibus res Domitiani imperatoris composui." The two contained together thirty books, as we learn from S. Jerome on Zachariah, ch. XIII., and related the events of about 70 years from the death of Augustus to the accession of Nerva. It is probable that Tacitus found it expedient to abandon the intention, announced in *Hist.* I. 1, of writing the history of the reigns of Nerva and Trajan. The records of an extinct dynasty furnished a subject 'less anxious' if not 'more fertile.' Accordingly we find him (*Ann.* III. 24) resolved, if his life should be prolonged, to choose another theme in a still earlier period, the reign of Augustus.

The letters addressed by the younger Pliny to Tacitus are the following : I. 6, 20 ; IV. 13 ; VI. 9, 16, 20 ; VII. 20, 33 ; VIII. 7 ; IX. 10, 14. Of these the one numbered IX. 10 has been ascribed, and not without probability, to Tacitus himself. In IX. 23, Pliny tells an interesting anecdote illustrative of the literary reputation which Tacitus had attained.

The style of the Ciceronian age aimed at richness of expression, and smoothly flowing and gracefully finished periods. It had been brought by Cicero to perhaps as high a degree of perfection as the Latin language permitted. The succeeding age proposed to itself a somewhat different aim. It wanted something *piquant* and stimulating.

Hence quite a different set of literary characteristics. A style sententious and concise, sometimes unpleasantly abrupt, with far-fetched, poetical and even archaic terms and expressions became fashionable. Scope was thus given to some of the worst extravagances of bad taste, and we find nearly all the writers of what is called the silver age indulging in pedantries and affectations which frequently render them harsh and obscure. A re-action followed in favour of the earlier or Ciceronian style. Of this we have evident traces in Tacitus. He seems to have aimed at combining some of Cicero's most conspicuous graces with the pointed and sententious character of the new style. Though he occasionally wants clearness and perhaps strains too much after effect, he is on the whole a far more natural and straightforward writer than most of his contemporaries.

It has been usual to regard Cicero as the representative of the most perfect Latinity, and Tacitus as a man of genius belonging to a declining age and infected by many of its chief literary vices. This view ignores several important considerations and requires some correction. It is true that the style of Cicero, from its general conformity to certain precise and definite rules, is fitted to be a model of Latinity in a sense in which that of Tacitus cannot be. A modern scholar feels instinctively that the first is much more suitable for imitation, but it is, we think, a great mistake to claim on this ground for Cicero a distinct superiority over Tacitus. Cicero indeed was enabled by his great abilities and wide culture to give a richness and flexibility to the Latin language which it had not known before his time, and we may venture to affirm that without him there could not have been a Tacitus. If, however, we are to measure excellence of style by its capacity of adequately representing the profound and subtle ideas of a really great thinker, we shall see good reason for placing Tacitus in at least as high a rank as Cicero. In vividness of imagination, in insight into the intricacies of human character, in the breadth and comprehensiveness of his historical faculty, he stands first among Roman writers. These qualities are continually reflected in his style. In the language of the time, permeated as it was with Greek ideas and phrases, he found an instrument ready to his hand, he used it with a consummate mastery of its various resources, and succeeded in giving to great thoughts a singularly characteristic expression.

INTRODUCTION TO THE LIFE OF AGRICOLA.

THE Life of Agricola is the most perfect specimen we possess of ancient biography. It was written, we are told, in a spirit of filial affection to commemorate the virtues of a good man and the successes of a great general. All that was most characteristic of a Roman of the highest type found a place in Agricola. An able officer, a just and at the same time a popular governor, a vigorous reformer of abuses, a conqueror of hitherto unknown regions, he was also a man of mental culture, and of singular gentleness and amiability. He had every quality which could attract the sympathy and admiration of his son-in-law. The present work was no doubt intended to be something more than the customary 'laudatio' which was pronounced in memory of an eminent man, though its style, resembling occasionally that of the orator rather than the historian, shows it to have been of a kindred character. It was designed as a κτῆμα ἐς ἀεὶ, in which it might be felt that a record of the achievements of Roman arms was happily blended with an affectionate testimony to individual worth and distinction. For English readers, its purpose has been thoroughly fulfilled. Its bearing on one of the earliest passages of our history must always make it of interest to us.

Besides a description of the geography of Britain and of the general character of its inhabitants, in accordance with the best information which Tacitus could procure, we have also a brief outline of the Roman operations in the country previous to Agricola's arrival. The actual subjugation of Britain and its formation into a province cannot be said to have been even attempted earlier than the reign of Claudius. It had indeed been twice invaded by Caesar in B.C. 55 and 54, but Caesar, as Tacitus observes, was rather the discoverer than the conqueror of the island. During the reigns of Augustus, Tiberius and Caligula Britain was left to itself. In A.D. 43 an expedition was undertaken by the direction of the emperor Claudius under the command of Aulus Plautius who seems to have advanced as far as the northern bank of the Thames and with Vespasian as his legatus to have gained a firm footing for the Romans. In the following year Claudius invaded Britain in person and defeated one of its most powerful tribes, the Trinobantes, who occupied Hertford and Essex. This success was followed by the submission of the Regni in Sussex and of the Iceni in Norfolk and Suffolk. Plautius was

succeeded by Ostorius Scapula in A.D. 47, by whom
the military colony of Camulodunum (Colchester) was
established in A.D. 50. From this time the southern
part of Britain (proxima pars Britanniae) may be considered to have been reduced to the form of a province.
Camulodunum was practically the capital. Succeeding
governors did little to extend the Roman dominion.
In A.D. 61 the province was all but lost. The Iceni
under Boudicea suddenly rose in rebellion, stormed
Camulodunum and massacred its garrison. They were
however completely beaten by Suetonius Paulinus,
the governor, and the southern Britons were effectually reconquered while the northern were overawed.
During the following years the country was gradually
Romanised, and the colonies of Camulodunum, Verulamium and Londinium which had been destroyed in
the insurrection of Boudicea recovered their position.
Vespasian's reign from A.D. 69 to 79, saw the work of
conquest still further advanced under Cerialis and his
successor Frontinus. The Silures in South Wales and
the Brigantes in Yorkshire yielded to the Roman
arms. Agricola, who had served with credit under
Cerialis and who became proconsul of Britain A.D. 78,
in succession to Frontinus, found on his arrival by far
the greater portion of the country already conquered,
though much remained to be done to secure thoroughly
the submission of the people.

The chief interest of this biography is evidently
intended to centre in the grand event of the seventh
year of Agricola's campaigns, the defeat of the con-

federate Caledonian tribes by which the subjugation
of Britain to its furthest limits was finally achieved.
The description of the preparations for the battle and
of the battle itself would occupy a space altogether
out of proportion to the rest of the work were it not
meant by the author to claim the first place in the
interest of his readers. Both the scene and the event
appear to have deeply impressed the mind of Tacitus.
The critical struggle, as it seemed to him, was fought
out on the last confines of the world, and it added to
the glory of Rome the renown of a triumph which
completed the conquest of her most inaccessible and
intractable province. The speeches of the rival
generals which introduce it, are elaborate specimens
of Tacitean eloquence. That of the Caledonian chief
is conceived in the true spirit of the barbarian and is
marked by a fierce impetuosity; that of Agricola is
calm and dignified, and implies the consciousness of
superior strength, which is the fruit of discipline and
civilisation.

Soon after his decisive success, which excited the
jealousy and ill-will of Domitian, Agricola returned to
Rome. Of the last eight years of his life, which were
passed in retirement, Tacitus tells us but little. In a
few burning words he dwells on the horrors of the
closing period of Domitian's reign and hints, though he
forbears explicitly to assert, as Dion Cassius does, that
Agricola was one of the Emperor's numerous victims.

The text of the Agricola presents many difficulties.
In three or four passages it is probably hopelessly

corrupt. Great critical acumen has been brought to
bear on it by Wex, who in the Prolegomena to his
edition, published 1852, has discussed the entire subject of the MSS. as well as every controverted passage
at great length. He thinks meanly of the recension
of Puteolanus in the 15th century, on which the
common reading of the text has from that time been
based. He relies chiefly on one of the Vatican MSS.
of the 15th century, the work of Pomponius Laetus
and containing on the margin the various readings of
another MS. which are written in the same hand.
Wex's examination of this MS. is subsequent to
that of Orelli and Baiter. Of recent editors he has
done the most for the Agricola. The more recent
edition of Kritz mainly owes its value to Wex.

Table of Passages in which the Text of this Edition of the Agricola differs from that of Orelli.

	ORELLI.	C. AND B.
Ch. IV.	Caesarum	Caesaris
	pater [Julii]	pater fuit
V.	exercitatior	excitatior
X.	unde et univèrsis fama est transgressa	unde et in universum fama est transgressa
	quam † hactenus jussum et hiems abdebat	quia hactenus jussum et hiems appetebat
XI.	habitasse	occupasse
	persuasione	persuasiones
XIII.	† auctoritate operis	auctor iterati operis
XV.	manus	manum
XVIII.	ad occasionem uterentur	ad occasionem verterentur
XIX.	nescire	ascire
XX.	tanta	et tanta
XXI.	in bella	bello
XXII.	ad Taum	ad Tanaum
	nihil superest; secretum et silentium ejus non timeres	nihil superest secretum, ut silentium ejus non timeres
XXV.	oppugnasse	oppugnare
XXVII.	Britanni † non virtute sed occasione et arte ducis rati	Britanni non virtute sed occasione et arte ducis elusos rati
XXVIII.	mox ad aquam atque ut illa raptis secum plerisque	mox ad aquam atque utilia rapientes cum plerisque

	ORELLI.	C. AND B.
XXX.	totius Britanniae	toti Britanniae
XXXI.	bona fortunasque in tributum aggerant, annum in frumentum, corpora ipsa ac manus silvis ac paludibus emuniendis inter verbera ac contumelias conterunt	bona fortunaeque in tributum, ager atque annus in frumentum, corpora ipsa ac manus silvis ac paludibus emuniendis inter verbera et contumelias conteruntur
XXXII.	nisi si	nisi
	infirma vincla caritatis	infirma vincla loco caritatis
XXXV.	bellanti	bellandi
	in aequo	aequo
	convexi	connexi
	covinnarius et eques	covinnarius eques
XXXVI.	tres Batavorum cohortes	Batavorum cohortes
	commixtae	connisae
	minimeque † equestres. Ea enim pugnae facies erat, cum aegra diu aut stante simul equorum	minimeque equestris ea jam pugnae facies erat, quum aegre clivo instantes simul equorum
XLI.	cum formidine eorum	cum formidine ceterorum
XLII.	iturusne esset	iturusne esset in provinciam
XLIII.	statim oblitus est	statim oblitus. Et...
XLIV.	excessit sexto et quinquagesimo anno	excessit quarto et quinquagesimo anno
	in hac beatissimi seculi luce	in hanc beatissimi seculi lucem
XLV.	Massa Boebius jam tum reus erat	Massa Boebius tum reus erat
	nobis tam longae absentiae	nobis tum longae absentiae
XLVI.	oblivio obruet	oblivio obruit

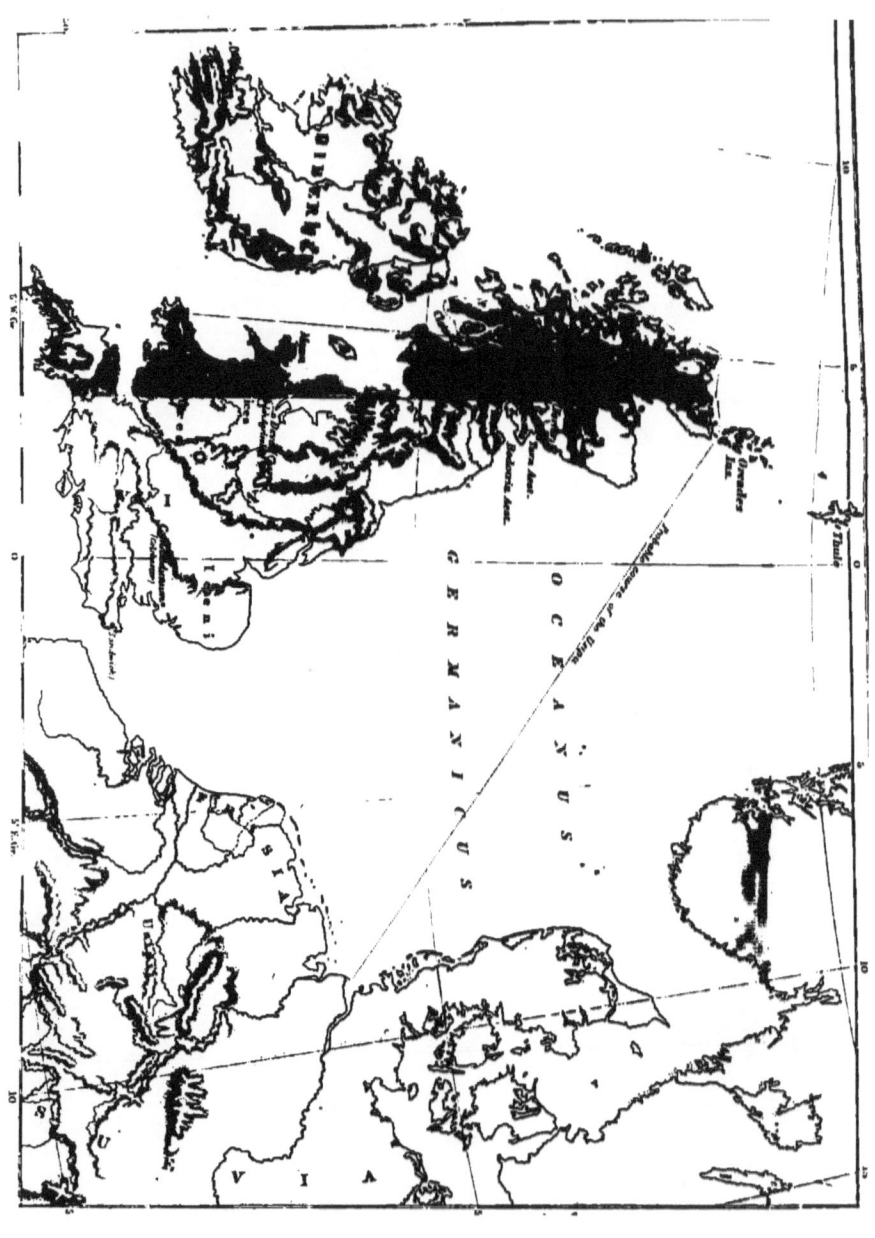

VITA

GNAEI JULII AGRICOLAE.

I.—III. Tacitus apologises for offering biography to an age which, though better and more hopeful than the terrible period of Domitian, was still so far demoralised as to prefer satires on vice to the praises of virtue.

I. Clarorum virorum facta moresque posteris tradere, antiquitus usitatum, ne nostris quidem temporibus quamquam incuriosa suorum, aetas omisit, quotiens magna aliqua ac nobilis virtus vicit ac supergressa est vitium parvis magnisque civitatibus commune, ignorantiam recti et invidiam. Sed apud priores ut agere digna memoratu pronum magisque in aperto erat, ita celeberrimus quisque ingenio ad prodendam virtutis memoriam sine gratia aut ambitione bonae tantum conscientiae pretio ducebatur. Ac plerique suam ipsi vitam narrare fiduciam potius morum quam arrogantiam arbitrati sunt, nec id Rutilio et Scauro citra fidem aut obtrectationi fuit; adeo virtutes iisdem temporibus optime aestimantur, quibus facillime gignuntur. At nunc narraturo mihi vitam defuncti hominis venia opus fuit; quam non petissem incusaturus tam saeva et infesta virtutibus tempora

T.A.   1

II. Legimus, quum Aruleno Rustico Paetus Thrasea, Herennio Senecioni Priscus Helvidius laudati essent, capitale fuisse, neque in ipsos modo auctores, sed in libros quoque eorum saevitum, delegato triumviris ministerio, ut monumenta clarissimorum ingeniorum in comitio ac foro urerentur. Scilicet illo igne vocem populi Romani et libertatem senatus et conscientiam generis humani aboleri arbitrabantur, expulsis insuper sapientiae professoribus atque omni bona arte in exilium acta, ne quid usquam honestum occurreret. Dedimus profecto grande patientiae documentum; et sicut vetus aetas vidit, quid ultimum in libertate esset, ita nos, quid in servitute, adempto per inquisitiones etiam loquendi audiendique commercio. Memoriam quoque ipsam cum voce perdidissemus, si tam in nostra potestate esset oblivisci quam tacere.

III. Nunc demum redit animus; et quamquam primo statim beatissimi seculi ortu Nerva Caesar res olim dissociabiles miscuerit, principatum ac libertatem, augeatque quotidie felicitatem temporum Nerva Traianus, nec spem modo ac votum Securitas publica, sed ipsius voti fiduciam ac robur assumpserit, natura tamen infirmitatis humanae tardiora sunt remedia quam mala; et ut corpora nostra lente augescunt, cito extinguuntur, sic ingenia studiaque oppresseris facilius quam revocaveris. Subit quippe etiam ipsius inertiae dulcedo, et invisa primo desidia postremo amatur. Quid? si per quindecim annos, grande mortalis aevi spatium, multi fortuitis casibus, promptissimus quisque saevitia principis interciderunt, pauci, et, uti dixerim, non modo aliorum, sed etiam nostri superstites sumus, exemptis e media vita tot annis, quibus iuvenes ad senectutem, senes prope ad ipsos exactae

aetatis terminos per silentium venimus. Non tamen
pigebit vel incondita ac rudi voce memoriam prioris
servitutis ac testimonium praesentium bonorum com-
posuisse. Hic interim liber, honori Agricolae soceri
mei destinatus, professione pietatis aut laudatus erit
aut excusatus.

IV.—VII. A. D. 40.—A. D. 70. *Agricola's birth, parent-*
age and education. He serves his military appren-
ticeship in Britain under Suetonius Paullinus at
a peculiarly critical time. His marriage. He be-
comes Quaestor and Praetor. Death of his mother.
He joins the cause of Vespasian, is appointed to
the command of the 20th legion in Britain, and ac-
quits himself with credit.

IV. Gnaeus Iulius Agricola, vetere et illustri
Foroiuliensium colonia ortus, utrumque avum pro-
curatorem Caesaris habuit, quae equestris nobilitas est.
Pater fuit Iulius Graecinus senatorii ordinis, studio
eloquentiae sapientiaeque notus, iisque ipsis virtutibus
iram Gaii Caesaris meritus; namque M. Silanum accusare iussus, et, quia abnuerat, interfectus est. Mater
Iulia Procilla fuit, rarae castitatis. In huius sinu
indulgentiaque educatus per omnem honestarum artium cultum pueritiam adolescentiamque transegit.
Arcebat eum ab illecebris peccantium, praeter ipsius
bonam integramque naturam, quod statim parvulus
sedem ac magistram studiorum Massiliam habuit,
locum Graeca comitate et provinciali parsimonia mis-
tum ac bene compositum. Memoria teneo solitum
ipsum narrare se prima in iuventa studium philo-
sophiae acrius, ultra quam concessum Romano ac
senatori, hausisse, ni prudentia matris incensum ac
flagrantem animum coërcuisset. Scilicet sublime et

1—2

erectum ingenium pulchritudinem ac speciem magnae excelsaeque gloriae vehementius quam caute appetc· bat. Mox mitigavit ratio et aetas, retinuitque, quod est difficillimum, ex sapientia modum.

V. Prima castrorum rudimenta in Britannia Suetonio Paulino, diligenti ac moderato duci, approbavit electus, quem contubernio aestimaret. Nec Agricola licenter, more iuvenum, qui militiam in lasciviam vertunt, neque segniter ad voluptates et commeatus titulum tribunatus et inscitiam rettulit; sed noscere provinciam, nosci exercitui, discere a peritis, sequi optimos, nihil appetere in iactationem, nihil ob formidinem recusare, simulque et anxius et intentus agere. Non sane alias excitatior magisque in ambiguo Britannia fuit. Trucidati veterani, incensae coloniae, intersepti exercitus; tum de salute, mox de victoria certavere. Quae cuncta etsi consiliis ductuque alterius agebantur, ac summa rerum et recuperatae provinciae gloria in ducem cessit, artem et usum et stimulos addidere iuveni, intravitque animum militaris gloriae cupido, ingrata temporibus, quibus sinistra erga eminentes interpretatio, nec minus periculum ex magna fama quam ex mala.

VI. Hinc ad capessendos magistratus in urbem digressus Domitiam Decidianam, splendidis natalibus ortam, sibi iunxit, idque matrimonium ad maiora nitenti decus ac robur fuit. Vixeruntque mira concordia per mutuam caritatem et invicem se anteponendo, nisi quod in bona uxore tanto maior laus, quanto in mala plus culpae est. Sors quaesturae provinciam Asiam, proconsulem Salvium Titianum dedit. Quorum neutro corruptus est, quamquam et provincia dives ac parata peccantibus, et proconsul in omnem

aviditatem pronus quantalibet facilitate redempturus
esset mutuam dissimulationem mali. Auctus est ibi
filia, in subsidium simul et solatium ; nam filium ante
sublatum brevi amisit. Mox inter quaesturam ac
tribunatum plebis atque ipsum etiam tribunatus annum quiete et otio transiit, gnarus sub Nerone temporum, quibus inertia pro sapientia fuit. Idem prae-
turae tenor et silentium ; nec enim iurisdictio obvenerat. Ludos et inania honoris medio rationis atque
abundantiae duxit, uti longe a luxuria, ita famae
propior. Tum electus a Galba ad dona templorum
recognoscenda, diligentissima conquisitione fecit, ne
cuius alterius sacrilegium res publica quam Neronis
sensisset.

VII. Sequens annus gravi vulnere animum do-
mumque eius afflixit. Nam classis Othoniana licenter
vaga, dum Intemelios (Liguriae pars est) hostiliter
populatur, matrem Agricolae in praediis suis interfecit,
praediaque ipsa et magnam patrimonii partem diripuit,
quae caussa caedis fuerat. Igitur ad sollemnia pietatis
profectus Agricola nuntio affectati a Vespasiano imperii deprehensus, ac statim in partes transgressus est.
Initia principatus ac statum urbis Mucianus regebat,
iuvene admodum Domitiano, et ex paterna fortuna
tantum licentiam usurpante. Is missum ad delectus
agendos Agricolam integreque ac strenue versatum
vicesimae legioni, tarde ad sacramentum transgressae,
praeposuit, ubi decessor seditiose agere narrabatur ;
quippe legatis quoque consularibus nimia ac for-
midolosa erat, nec legatus praetorius ad cohibendum
potens, incertum, suo an militum ingenio. Ita successor simul et ultor electus rarissima moderatione
maluit videri invenisse bonos quam fecisse.

VIII. IX. A.D. 70.—A.D. 78. *Singular tact of Agricola. He is appointed by Vespasian governor of Aquitania, is recalled to Rome to be made consul, and on the expiration of his consulate, becomes governor of Britain.*

VIII. Praeerat tunc Britanniae Vettius Bolanus, placidius quam feroci provincia dignum est. Temperavit Agricola vim suam, ardoremque compescuit, ne incresceret, peritus obsequi eruditusque utilia honestis miscere. Brevi deinde Britannia consularem Petilium Cerialem accepit. Habuerunt virtutes spatium exemplorum. Sed primo Cerialis labores modo et discrimina, mox et gloriam communicabat; saepe parti exercitus in experimentum, aliquando maioribus copiis ex eventu praefecit. Nec Agricola umquam in suam famam gestis exsultavit; ad auctorem ac ducem ut minister fortunam referebat. Ita virtute in obsequendo, verecundia in praedicando extra invidiam nec extra gloriam erat.

IX. Revertentem ab legatione legionis divus Vespasianus inter patricios ascivit, ac deinde provinciae Aquitaniae praeposuit, splendidae imprimis dignitatis administratione ac spe consulatus, cui destinarat. Credunt plerique militaribus ingeniis subtilitatem deesse, quia castrensis iurisdictio secura et obtusior ac plura manu agens calliditatem fori non exerceat. Agricola naturali prudentia, quamvis inter togatos, facile iusteque agebat. Iam vero tempora curarum remissionumque divisa; ubi conventus ac iudicia poscerent, gravis, intentus, severus, et saepius misericors; ubi officio satisfactum, nulla ultra potestatis persona. Tristitiam et arrogantiam et avaritiam exuerat; nec illi, quod est rarissimum, aut facilitas

auctoritatem aut severitas amorem deminuit. In-
tegritatem atque abstinentiam in tanto viro referre
iniuria virtutum fuerit. Ne famam quidem, cui saepe
etiam boni indulgent, ostentanda virtute aut per artem
quaesivit; procul ab aemulatione adversus collegas,
procul a contentioue adversus procuratores, et vincere
inglorium et atteri sordidum arbitrabatur. Minus
triennium in ea legatione detentus ac statim ad spem
consulatus revocatus est, comitante opinione Britanniam ei provinciam dari, nullis in hoc suis sermonibus,
sed quia par videbatur. Haud semper errat fama;
aliquando et elegit. Consul egregiae tum spei filiam
iuveni mihi despondit, ac post consulatum collocavit;
et statim Britanniae praepositus est, adiecto pontifi-
catus sacerdotio.

x.—xii. *Britain; its boundaries, shape, surrounding
seas, origin, character, customs of its inhabitants;
climate, products of the soil.*

X. Britanniae situm populosque multis scriptoribus memoratos non in comparationem curae ingeniive
referam, sed quia tum primum perdomita est; ita,
quae priores nondum comperta eloquentia percoluere,
rerum fide tradentur. Britannia, insularum, quas
Romana notitia complectitur, maxima, spatio ac coelo
in orientem Germaniae, in occidentem Hispaniae obtenditur; Gallis in meridiem etiam inspicitur. Septentrionalia eius, nullis contra terris, vasto atque
aperto mari pulsantur. Formam totius Britanniae
Livius veterum Fabius Rusticus recentium eloquen-
tissimi auctores oblongae scutulae vel bipenni assi-
milavere. Et est ea facies citra Caledoniam, unde et

in universum fama est transgressa. Sed immensum
et euorme spatium procurrentium extremo iam litore
terrarum velut in cuneum tenuatur.   Hanc oram
novissimi maris tunc primum Romana classis circum-
vecta insulam esse Britanniam affirmavit, ac simul
incognitas ad id tempus insulas, quas Orcadas vocant,
invenit domuitque.   Dispecta est et Thule, quia hactenus iussum, et hiems appetebat.   Sed mare pigrum
et grave remigantibus ; perhibent ne ventis quidem
proinde attolli ; credo, quod rariores terrae montesque,
caussa ac materia tempestatum, et profunda moles
continui maris tardius impellitur.   Naturam Oceani
atque aestus neque quaerere huius operis est, ac multi
rettulere.   Unum addiderim, nusquam latius dominari
mare, multum fluminum huc atque illuc ferre, nec
litore tenus accrescere aut resorberi, sed influere
penitus atque ambire, et iugis etiam ac montibus inseri
velut in suo.

XI.   Ceterum Britanniam qui mortales initio
coluerint, indigenae an advecti, ut inter barbaros,
parum compertum.   Habitus corporum varii, atque
ex eo argumenta.   Namque rutilae Caledoniam habi-
tantium comae, magni artus Germanicam originem
asseverant.   Silurum colorati vultus, torti plerumque
crines, et posita contra Hispania Iberos veteres traie-
cisse easque sedes occupasse fidem faciunt.   Proximi
Gallis et similes sunt, seu durante originis vi, seu
procurrentibus in diversa terris positio coeli corporibus
habitum dedit.   In universum tamen aestimanti Gallos
vicinam insulam occupasse credibile est.   Eorum sacra
deprehendas, superstitionum persuasiones ; sermo haud
multum diversus ; in deposcendis periculis eadem
audacia, et, ubi advenere, in detrectandis eadem for-

mido. Plus tamen ferociae Britanni praeferunt, ut
quos nondum longa pax emollierit. Nam Gallos quoque in bellis floruisse accepimus; mox segnitia cum
otio intravit, amissa virtute pariter ac libertate.
Quod Britannorum olim victis evenit; ceteri manent,
quales Galli fuerunt.

XII. In pedite robur; quaedam nationes et curru
proeliantur; honestior auriga, clientes propugnant.
Olim regibus parebant, nunc per principes factionibus
et studiis trahuntur, nec aliud adversus validissimas
gentes pro nobis utilius quam quod in commune non
consulunt. Rarus duabus tribusque civitatibus ad
propulsandum commune periculum conventus; ita
singuli pugnant, universi vincuntur. Coelum crebris
imbribus ac nebulis foedum; asperitas frigorum abest.
Dierum spatia ultra nostri orbis mensuram; nox clara
et extrema Britanniae parte brevis, ut finem atque
initium lucis exiguo discrimine internoscas. Quod si
nubes non officiant, aspici per noctem solis fulgorem,
nec occidere et exsurgere sed transire affirmant. Scilicet extrema et plana terrarum humili umbra non
erigunt tenebras, infraque coelum et sidera nox cadit.
Solum, praeter oleam vitemque et cetera calidioribus
terris oriri sueta, patiens frugum, fecundum; tarde
mitescunt, cito proveniunt, eademque utriusque rei
caussa, multus humor terrarum coelique. Fert Britannia aurum et argentum et alia metalla, pretium
victoriae. Gignit et oceanus margarita, sed subfusca
ac liventia. Quidam artem abesse legentibus arbi-
trantur; nam in rubro mari viva ac spirantia saxis
avelli, in Britannia, prout expulsa sint, colligi. Ego
facilius crediderim naturam margaritis deesse quam
nobis avaritiam.

XIII.—XVII.   *Sketch of the Roman conquest of Britain
from the invasion of Julius Caesar to its more
complete subjugation by Claudius.   Roman governors of Britain.   Insurrection of the Britons under
Boadicea; they storm Camalodunum, but are completely defeated by Suetonius Paullinus.   Governors
who succeeded Paullinus.   Little done by them to
advance the Roman dominion in Britain. Vigorous
policy of Vespasian.*

XIII.   Ipsi Britanni delectum ac tributa et in-
iuncta imperii munera impigre obeunt, si iniuriae
absint; has aegre tolerant, iam domiti ut pareant,
nondum ut serviant. Igitúr primus omnium Roma-
norum divus Iulius cum exercitu Britanniam ingressus, quamquam prospera pugna terruerit incolas,
ac litore potitus sit, potest videri ostendisse posteris,
non tradidisse.   Mox bella civilia, et in rem publicam
versa principum arma, ac longa oblivio Britanniae
etiam in pace.   Consilium id divus Augustus vocabat,
Tiberius praeceptum. Agitasse Gaium Caesarem de
intranda Britannia satis constat, ni velox ingenio
mobilis poenitentiae, et ingentes adversus Germaniam
conatus frustra fuissent. Divus Claudius auctor iterati
operis, transvectis legionibus auxiliisque et assumpto
in partem rerum Vespasiano; quod initium venturae
mox fortunae fuit. Domitae gentes, capti reges, et
monstratus fatis Vespasianus.

XIV.   Consularium primus Aulus Plautius praepositus, ac subinde Ostorius Scapula, uterque bello
egregius; redactaque paulatim in formam provinciae
proxima pars Britanniae. Addita insuper vetera-
norum colonia.   Quaedam civitates Cogidumno regi
donatae (is ad nostram usque memoriam fidissimus

mansit), ut, vetere ac iam pridem recepta populi Romani consuetudine, haberet instrumenta servitutis et
reges. Mox Didius Gallus parta a prioribus continuit,
paucis admodum castellis in ulteriora promotis, per
quae fama aucti officii quaereretur. Didium Veranius
excepit, isque intra annum extinctus est. Suetonius
hinc Paulinus biennio prosperas res habuit subactis
nationibus firmatisque praesidiis; quorum fiducia
Monam insulam, ut vires rebellibus ministrantem,
aggressus terga occasioni patefecit.

XV. Namque absentia legati remoto metu,
Britanni agitare inter se mala servitutis, conferre
iniurias et interpretando accendere. Nihil profici
patientia, nisi ut graviora tamquam ex facili toleran-
tibus imperentur. Singulos sibi olim reges fuisse,
nunc binos imponi, e quibus legatus in sanguinem,
procurator in bona saeviret. Aeque discordiam prae-
positorum, aeque concordiam subiectis exitiosam;
alterius manum, centuriones, alterius servos vim et
contumelias miscere. Nihil iam cupiditati, nihil
libidini exceptum. In proelio fortiorem esse, qui
spoliet; nunc ab ignavis plerumque et imbellibus
eripi domos, abstrahi liberos, iniungi delectus, tamquam mori tantum pro patria nescientibus. Quantulum enim transisse militum, si sese Britanni numerent?
Sic Germanias excussisse iugum, et flumine, non oceano
defendi; sibi patriam, coniuges, parentes, illis avaritiam et luxuriam caussas belli esse. Recessuros, ut
divus Iulius recessisset, modo virtutem maiorum
suorum aemularentur. Neve proelii unius aut alterius
eventu pavescerent; plus impetus, maiorem constantiam penes miseros esse. Iam Britannorum etiam
deos misereri, qui Romanum ducem absentem, qui

relegatum in alia insula exercitum detinerent: iam ipsos, quod difficillimum fuerit, deliberare. Porro in eiusmodi consiliis periculosius esse deprehendi quam audere.

XVI. His atque talibus invicem instincti, Boudicea, generis regii femina, duce (neque enim sexum in imperiis discernunt) sumpsere universi bellum; ac sparsos per castella milites consectati, expugnatis praesidiis ipsam coloniam invasere ut sedem servitutis. Nec ullum in barbaris saevitiae genus omisit ira et victoria. Quod nisi Paulinus cognito provinciae motu propere subvenisset, amissa Britannia foret; quam unius proelii fortuna veteri patientiae restituit, (tenentibus arma plerisque, quos conscientia defectionis et propius ex legato timor agitabat), ni quamquam egregius cetera arroganter in deditos, et, ut suae cuiusque iniuriae ultor, durius consuleret. Missus igitur Petronius Turpilianus tamquam exorabilior et delictis hostium novus eoque poenitentiae mitior, compositis prioribus nihil ultra ausus Trebellio Maximo provinciam tradidit. Trebellius segnior et nullis castrorum experimentis comitate quadam curandi provinciam tenuit. Didicere iam barbari quoque ignoscere vitiis blandientibus, et interventus civilium armorum praebuit iustam segnitiae excusationem. Sed discordia laboratum, quum assuetus expeditionibus miles otio lasciviret. Trebellius, fuga ac latebris vitata exercitus ira indecorus atque humilis, precario mox praefuit, ac velut pacti exercitus licentiam, dux salutem; et seditio sine sanguine stetit. Nec Vettius Bolanus, manentibus adhuc civilibus bellis, agitavit Britanniam disciplina. Eadem inertia erga hostes, similis petulantia castrorum, nisi quod innocens

Bolanus et nullis delictis invisus caritatem paraverat
loco auctoritatis.

XVII. Sed ubi cum cetero orbe Vespasianus et
Britanniam recuperavit, magni duces, egregii exercitus,
minuta hostium spes. Et terrorem statim intulit
Petilius Cerialis, Brigantum civitatem, quae numero-
sissima provinciae totius perhibetur, aggressus. Multa
proelia, et aliquando non incruenta; magnamque
Brigantum partem aut victoria amplexus est aut
bello. Et Cerialis quidem alterius successoris curam famamque obruisset sed sustinuit molem Iulius
Frontinus, vir magnus, quantum licebat, validamque et
pugnacem Silurum gentem armis subegit, super virtutem hostium locorum quoque difficultates eluctatus.

XVIII.—XXI. A. D. 78.—A. D. 79. *Successes of Agricola in*
Britain. Defeat of the Ordovices. Attack on the
island of Mona. Terror and submission of the
Britons. Moderation and equity of Agricola's go-
vernment. His reform of abuses. He establishes forts
and garrisons, and introduces Roman civilization.

XVIII Hunc Britanniae statum, has bellorum
vices media iam aestate transgressus Agricola invenit,
quum et milites velut omissa expeditione ad securitatem, et hostes ad occasionem verterentur. Ordo-
vicum civitas haud multo ante adventum eius alam in
finibus suis agentem prope universam obtriverat,
eoque initio erecta provincia; et quibus bellum volentibus erat, probare exemplum, ac recentis legati
animum opperiri, quum Agricola, quamquam transvecta aestas, sparsi per provinciam numeri, praesumpta
apud militem illius anni quies, tarda et contraria
bellum inchoaturo, et plerisque custodiri suspecta
potius videbatur, ire obviam discrimini statuit; con-

tractisque legionum vexillis et modica auxiliorum manu, quia in aequum degredi Ordovices non audebant, ipse ante agmen, quo ceteris par animus simili periculo esset, erexit aciem. Caesaque prope universa gente, non ignarus instandum famae, ac, prout prima cessissent, terrorem ceteris fore, Monam insulam, cuius possessione revocatum Paulinum rebellione totius Britanniae supra memoravi, redigere in potestatem animo intendit. Sed, ut in dubiis consiliis, naves deerant; ratio et constantia ducis transvexit. Depositis omnibus sarcinis lectissimos auxiliarium, quibus nota vada et patrius nandi usus, quo simul seque et arma et equos regunt, ita repente immisit, ut obstupefacti hostes, qui classem, qui naves, qui mare exspectabant, nihil arduum aut invictum crediderint sic ad bellum venientibus. Ita petita pace ac dedita insula clarus ac magnus haberi Agricola, quippe cui ingredienti provinciam, quod tempus alii per ostentationem et officiorum ambitum transigunt, labor et periculum placuisset. Nec Agricola prosperitate rerum in vanitatem usus expeditionem aut victoriam vocabat victos continuisse; ne laureatis quidem gesta prosecutus est. Sed ipsa dissimulatione famae famam auxit aestimantibus, quanta futuri spe tam magna tacuisset.

XIX. Ceterum animorum provinciae prudens, simulque doctus per aliena experimenta parum profici armis, si injuriae sequerentur, causas bellorum statuit excidere. A se suisque orsus primum domum suam coërcuit, quod plerisque haud minus arduum est quam provinciam regere. Nihil per libertos servosque publicae rei, non studiis privatis nec ex commendatione aut precibus centurionem, milites ascire, sed optimum

quemque fidissimum putare; omnia scire, non omnia
exsequi; parvis peccatis veniam, magnis severitatem
commodare, nec poena semper, sed saepius poenitentia
contentus esse; officiis et administrationibus potius
non peccaturos praeponere, quam damnare, quum
peccassent. Frumenti et tributorum exactionem
aequalitate munerum mollire, circumcisis, quae in
quaestum reperta ipso tributo gravius· tolerabantur.
Namque per ludibrium assidere clausis horreis et
emere ultro frumenta ac ludere pretio cogebantur;
devortia itinerum et longinquitas regionum indicebatur,
ut civitates, proximis hibernis, in remota et avia
deferrent, donec, quod omnibus in promptu erat, paucis
lucrosum fieret.

XX. Haec primo statim anno comprimendo egregiam famam paci circumdedit, quae vel incuria vel
intolerantia priorum haud minus quam bellum time-
batur. Sed ubi aestas advenit, contracto exercitu
multus in agmine, laudare modestiam, disiectos coër-
cere; loca castris ipse capere, aestuaria ac silvas ipse
praetentare; et nihil interim apud hostes quietum
pati, quominús subitis excursibus popularetur; atque
ubi satis terruerat, parcendo rursus irritamenta pacis
ostentare. Quibus rebus multae civitates, quae in
illum diem ex aequo egerant, datis obsidibus iram
posuere, et praesidiis castellisque circumdatae, et tanta
ratione curaque ut nulla ante Britanniae nova pars.

XXI. Illacessita transiit sequens hiems, salu-
berrimis consiliis absumpta. Namque ut homines dis-
persi ac rudes eoque bello faciles quieti et otio per
voluptates assuescerent, hortari privatim, adiuvare
publice, ut templa, fora, domos exstruerent, laudando
promptos et castigando segnes. Ita honoris aemulatio

pro necessitate erat. Iam vero principum filios liberalibus artibus erudire, et ingenia Britannorum studiis
Gallorum anteferre, ut, qui modo linguam Romanam
abnuebant, eloquentiam concupiscerent. Inde etiam
habitus nostri honor, et frequens toga, paulatimque
discessum ad delenimenta vitiorum, porticus et balnea
et conviviorum elegantiam ; idque apud imperitos
humanitas vocabatur, quum pars servitutis esset.

XXII.—XXIV. A. D. 80.—A. D. 82. *Agricola pushes his*
conquests as far north as the Tanaus and draws a
line of forts from the Clota to the Bodotria. He
crosses the Clota and posts some troops on the western
coast opposite Ireland. Description of Ireland.

XXII. Tertius expeditionum annus novas gentes
aperuit, vastatis usque ad Tanaum (aestuario nomen
est) nationibus. Qua formidine territi hostes quamquam conflictatum saevis tempestatibus exercitum
lacessere non ausi ; ponendisque insuper castellis spatium fuit. Annotabant periti non alium ducem opportunitates locorum sapientius legisse. Nullum ab Agricola positum castellum aut vi hostium expugnatum
aut pactione ac fuga desertum ; crebrae eruptiones ;
nam adversus moras obsidionis annuis copiis firmabantur. Ita intrepida ibi hiems, et sibi quisque
praesidio, irritis hostibus eoque desperantibus, quia
soliti plerumque damna aestatis hibernis eventibus
pensare tum aestate atque hieme iuxta pellebantur.
Nec Agricola umquam per alios gesta avidus intercepit ;
seu centurio seu praefectus, incorruptum facti testem
habebat. Apud quosdam acerbior in conviciis narrabatur ; ut erat comis bonis, ita adversus malos iniucundus. Ceterum ex iracundia nihil supererat secretum,

ut silentium eius non timeres; honestius putabat offendere quam odisse.

XXIII.   Quarta aestas obtinendis, quae percucurrerat, insumpta, ac, si virtus exercituum et Romani nominis gloria pateretur, inventus in ipsa Britannia terminus.   Namque Clota et Bodotria, diversi maris aestibus per immensum revectae, angusto terrarum spatio dirimuntur, quod tum praesidiis firmabatur; atque omnis propior sinus tenebatur, summotis velut in aliam insulam hostibus.

XXIV. Quinto expeditionum anno nave prima transgressus ignotas ad id tempus gentes crebris simul ac prosperis proeliis domuit, eamque partem Britanniae, quae Hiberniam aspicit, copiis instruxit, in spem magis quam ob formidinem, si quidem Hibernia medio inter Britanniam atque Hispaniam sita et Gallico quoque mari opportuna valentissimam imperii partem magnis invicem usibus miscuerit.   Spatium eius, si Britanniae comparetur, angustius, nostri maris insulas superat. Solum coelumque et ingenia cultusque hominum haud multum a Britannia differunt; melius aditus portusque per commercia et negotiatores cogniti.   Agricola expulsum seditione domestica unum ex regulis gentis exceperat, ac specie amicitiae in occasionem retinebat. Saepe ex eo audivi legione una et modicis auxiliis debellari obtinerique Hiberniam posse, idque etiam adversus Britanniam profuturum, si Romana ubique arma, et velut e conspectu libertas tolleretur.

XXV.—XXIX.   A.D. 83.—A.D. 84.   *Agricola undertakes an expedition by sea and land to the north of the Bodotria, and is met by a confederation of the Caledonian tribes who make a sudden and furious attack on the 9th legion, but are ultimately defeated.   They*

prepare however to renew the conflict. Strange adven-
tures of a Usipian cohort. Agricola advances as far
as the Grampian mountains, where he is met by the
assembled forces of the Caledonians under Galgacus.

XXV. Ceterum aestate, qua sextum officii annum
inchoabat, amplexus civitates trans Bodotriam sitas,
quia motus universarum ultra gentium et infesta
hostilis exercitus itinera timebantur, portus classe
exploravit. Quae ab Agricola primum assumpta in
partem virium sequebatur egregia specie, quum simul
terra simul mari bellum impelleretur, ac saepe iisdem
castris pedes equesque et nauticus miles misti copiis et
laetitia sua quisque facta, suos casus attollerent, ac
modo silvarum ac montium profunda, modo tempestatum ac fluctuum adversa, hinc terra et hostis, hinc
victus oceanus militari iactantia compararentur. Bri-
tannos quoque, ut ex captivis audiebatur, visa classis
obstupefaciebat, tamquam aperto maris sui secreto
ultimum victis perfugium clauderetur. Ad manus et
arma conversi Caledoniam incolentes populi paratu
magno, maiore fama, uti mos est de ignotis, oppugnare
ultro castellum adorti, metum ut provocantes addide-
rant; regrediendumque citra Bodotriam, et excedendum
potius quam pellerentur, ignavi specie prudentium
admonebant, quum interim cognoscit hostes pluribus
agminibus irrupturos. Ac ne superante numero et
peritia locorum circumiretur, diviso et ipse in tres
partes exercitu incessit.

XXVI. Quod ubi cognitum hosti, mutato repente
consilio universi nonam legionem, ut maxime invalidam, nocte aggressi, inter somnum ac trepidationem,
caesis vigilibus, irrupere. Iamque in ipsis castris
pugnabatur, quum Agricola, iter hostium ab ex-

ploratoribus edoctus et vestigiis insecutus, velocissi-
mos equitum peditumque assultare tergis pugnantium
iubet, mox ab universis adiici clamorem ; et propinqua
luce fulsere signa.   Ita ancipiti malo territi Britanni ;
et Romanis rediit animus, ac securi pro salute de
gloria certabant.   Ultro quin etiam erupere, et fuit
atrox in ipsis portarum angustiis proelium, donec pulsi
hostes, utroque exercitu certante, his, ut tulisse opem,
illis, ne eguisse auxilio viderentur.   Quod nisi paludes
et silvae fugientes texissent, debellatum illa victoria
foret.

XXVII.   Cuius conscientia ac fama ferox exercitus nihil virtuti suae invium, et penetrandam Caledoniam inveniendumque tandem Britanniae terminum
continuo proeliorum cursu fremebant ; atque illi modo
cauti ac sapientes prompti post eventum ac magniloqui
erant.   Iniquissima haec bellorum condicio est ; prospera omnes sibi vindicant, adversa uni imputantur.
At Britanni, non virtute, sed occasione et arte ducis
elusos rati, nihil ex arrogantia remittere, quominus
iuventutem armarent, coniuges ac liberos in loca tuta
transferrent, coetibus ac sacrificiis conspirationem civitatum sancirent.   Atque ita irritatis utrimque animis
discessum.

XXVIII.   Eadem aestate cohors Usipiorum per
Germanias conscripta et in Britanniam transmissa
magnum ac memorabile facinus ausa est.   Occiso centurione ac militibus, qui ad tradendam disciplinam
immisti manipulis exemplum et rectores habebantur,
tres liburnicas adactis per vim gubernatoribus as-
cendere ; et uno remigante, suspectis duobus eoque
interfectis, nondum vulgato rumore ut miraculum
praevehebantur.   Mox ad aquam atque utilia rapientes

2—2

cum plerisque Britannorum sua defensantium proelio congressi, ac saepe victores, aliquando pulsi, eo ad extremum inopiae venere, ut infirmissimos suorum, mox sorte ductos vescerentur.   Atque ita circumvecti Britanniam, amissis per inscitiam regendi navibus, pro praedonibus habiti, primum a Suevis, mox a Frisiis intercepti sunt.   Ac fuere, quos per commercia venundatos et in nostram usque ripam mutatione ementium adductos indicium tanti casus illustravit.

XXIX.   Initio aestatis Agricola domestico vulnere ictus.   Anno ante natum filium amisit; quem casum neque, ut plerique fortium virorum, ambitiose, neque per lamenta rursus ac maerorem muliebriter tulit.   Et in luctu bellum inter remedia erat.   Igitur praemissa classe, quae pluribus locis praedata magnum et incertum terrorem faceret, expedito exercitu, cui ex Britannis fortissimos et longa pace exploratos addiderat, ad montem Grampium pervenit, quem iam hostis insederat.   Nam Britanni, nihil fracti pugnae prioris eventu, et ultionem aut servitium exspectantes, tandemque docti commune periculum concordia propulsandum, legationibus et foederibus omnium civitatum vires exciverant.   Iamque super triginta milia armatorum aspiciebantur, et adhuc affluebat omnis iuventus et quibus cruda ac viridis senectus, clari bello et sua quisque decora gestantes, quum inter plures duces virtute et genere praestans, nomine Calgacus, apud contractam multitudinem proelium poscentem in hunc modum locutus fertur :

XXX.—XXXII.   *Speech of Galgacus to his army. He dwells on the urgency of the crisis, on the hopelessness of escape from the Roman lust of dominion, on the almost certain success which will attend the*

united efforts of a hitherto unconquered people, whose
freedom is threatened by a miscellaneous host of
invaders which is held together by fear and terror
rather than by fidelity and affection.

XXX. Quotiens caussas belli et necessitatem
nostram intueor, magnus mihi animus est hodiernum
diem consensumque vestrum initium libertatis toti
Britanniae fore. Nam et universi servitutis expertes,
et nullae ultra terrae, ac ne mare quidem securum
imminente nobis classe Romana. Ita proelium atque
arma, quae fortibus honesta, eadem etiam ignavis
tutissima sunt. Priores pugnae, quibus adversus
Romanos varia fortuna certatum est, spem ac subsidium
in nostris manibus habebant, quia nobilissimi totius
Britanniae, iique in ipsis penetralibus siti, nec servientium litora aspicientes, oculos quoque a contactu
dominationis inviolatos habebamus. Nos terrarum ac
libertatis extremos recessus ipse ac sinus famae in
hunc diem defendit, atque omne ignotum pro magnifico est. Sed nunc terminus Britanniae patet. Nulla
iam ultra gens, nihil nisi fluctus et saxa, et infestiores
Romani, quorum superbiam frustra per obsequium ac
modestiam effugeris. Raptores orbis, postquam cuncta
vastantibus defuere terrae, iam et mare scrutantur;
si locuples hostis est, avari, si pauper, ambitiosi, quos
non Oriens, non Occidens satiaverit. Soli omnium
opes atque inopiam pari affectu concupiscunt. Auferre,
trucidare, rapere falsis nominibus imperium, atque ubi
solitudinem faciunt, pacem appellant.

XXXI. Liberos cuique ac propinquos suos natura
carissimos esse voluit. Hi per delectus alibi servituri
auferuntur; coniuges sororesque, etiamsi hostilem
libidinem effugiant, nomine amicorum atque hospitum

polluuntur. Bona fortunaeque in tributum, ager atque
annus in frumentum, corpora ipsa ac manus silvis
ac paludibus emuniendis inter verbera ac contumelias
conteruntur. Nata servituti mancipia semel veneunt,
atque ultro a dominis aluntur; Britannia servitutem
suam quotidie emit, quotidie pascit. Ac sicut in
familia recentissimus quisque servorum etiam conservis
ludibrio est, sic in hoc orbis terrarum vetere famulatu
novi nos et viles in excidium petimur. Neque enim
arva nobis aut metalla aut portus sunt, quibus exer-
cendis reservemur. Virtus porro ac ferocia subiect-
orum ingrata imperantibus; et longinquitas ac secretum ipsum quo tutius, eo suspectius. Ita sublata
spe veniae tandem sumite animum, tam quibus salus
quam quibus gloria carissima est. Brigantes femina
duce exurere coloniam, expugnare castra, ac, nisi
felicitas in socordiam vertisset, exuere iugum potuere;
nos integri et indomiti et libertatem non in poenitentiam laturi, primo statim congressu ostendamus, quos
sibi Caledonia viros seposuerit.

XXXII. An eandem Romanis in bello virtutem
quam in pace lasciviam adesse creditis? Nostris
illi dissensionibus ac discordiis clari vitia hostium in
gloriam exercitus sui vertunt; quem contractum ex
diversissimis gentibus ut secundae res tenent, ita adversae dissolvent, nisi Gallos et Germanos et (pudet
dictu) Britannorum plerosque, licet dominationi alienae
sanguinem commodent, diutius tamen hostes quam
servos, fide et affectu teneri putatis. Metus ac terror
est, infirma vincla loco caritatis; quae ubi removeris,
qui timere desierint, odisse incipient. Omnia victoriae
incitamenta pro nobis sunt; nullae Romanos coniuges accendunt, nulli parentes fugam exprobraturi

suut; aut nulla plerisque patria aut alia est. Paucos
numero, trepidos ignorantia, coelum ipsum ac mare
et silvas, ignota omnia, circumspectantes, clausos quo-
dammodo ac vinctos dii nobis tradiderunt. Ne terreat
vanus aspectus et auri fulgor atque argenti, quod
neque tegit neque vulnerat. In ipsa hostium acie
inveniemus nostras manus; agnoscent Britanni suam
caussam, recordabuntur Galli priorem libertatem,
deserent illos ceteri Germani, tamquam nuper Usipii
relinquerunt. Nec quicquam ultra formidinis; vacua
castella, senum coloniae, inter male parentes et iniuste
imperantes aegra municipia et discordantia. Hic dux,
hic exercitus; illic tributa et metalla et ceterae servientium poenae, quas in aeternum perferre aut statim
ulcisci in hoc campo est. Proinde ituri in aciem et
maiores vestros et posteros cogitate.

XXXIII.—XXXIV. *Agricola's address to his troops. He
reminds them of the courage and endurance which
seven years' military service has tested, of the unique
character of their achievements, of their desperate position, of their glorious end, should they
be overpowered, in these remote and unexplored
regions. The enemy, he suggests, has stood his
ground rather under the influence of panic than of
steady deliberate bravery.*

XXXIII. Excepere orationem alacres, ut barbaris
moris, cantu fremituque et clamoribus dissonis. Iamque agmina, et armorum fulgores audentissimi cuiusque procursu; simul instruebatur acies, quum Agricola,
quamquam laetum et vix munimentis coërcitum
militem accendendum adhuc ratus, ita disseruit:

Octavus annus est, commilitones, ex quo virtute et
auspiciis imperii Romani, fide atque opera vestra

Britanniam vicistis. Tot expeditionibus, tot proeliis, seu fortitudine adversus hostes seu patientia ac labore paene adversus ipsam rerum naturam opus fuit, neque me militum neque vos ducis poenituit. Ergo egressi, ego veterum legatorum, vos priorum exercituum terminos, finem Britanniae non fama nec rumore, sed castris et armis tenemus. Inventa Britannia et subacta. Equidem saepe in agmine, quum vos paludes montesve et flumina fatigarent, fortissimi cuiusque voces audiebam : quando dabitur hostis, quando acies ? Veniunt, e latebris suis extrusi, et vota virtusque in aperto, omniaque prona victoribus, atque eadem victis adversa. Nam ut superasse tantum itineris, silvas evasisse, transisse aestuaria pulchrum ac decorum in frontem, ita fugientibus periculosissima, quae hodie prosperrima sunt. Neque enim nobis aut locorum eadem notitia aut commeatuum eadem abundantia, sed manus et arma, et in his omnia. Quod ad me attinet, iam pridem mihi decretum est neque exercitus neque ducis terga tuta esse. Proinde et honesta mors turpi vita potior, et incolumitas ac decus eodem loco sita sunt; nec inglorium fuerit in ipso terrarum ac naturae fine cecidisse.

XXXIV. Si novae gentes atque ignota acies constitisset, aliorum exercituum exemplis vos hortarer; nunc vestra decora recensete, vestros oculos interrogate. Hi sunt, quos proximo anno unam legionem furto noctis aggressos clamore debellastis; hi ceterorum Britannorum fugacissimi, ideoque tam diu superstites. Quomodo silvas saltusque penetrantibus fortissimum quodque animal contra ruere,—pavida et inertia ipso agminis sono pelluntur,—sic acerrimi Britannorum iam pridem ceciderunt, reliquus est numerus ignavorum et metuentium. Quos quod tandem invenistis, non restiterunt, sed deprehensi sunt; novissimae res et extremo metu corpora defixere aciem in his vestigiis, in quibus pulchram et spectabilem victoriam ederetis. Transigite cum expeditionibus, imponite quinquaginta annis magnum diem, approbate rei publicae nunquam exercitui imputari potuisse aut moras belli aut caussas rebellandi.

xxxv.—xxxix. *The order of battle. Desperate courage of the Britons. Their complete defeat. Loss on both sides. Terrible scenes on the battle-field. Expedition of the Roman fleet. Agricola returns southwards. Effect on Domitian of the news of Agricola's successes.*

XXXV. Et alloquente adhuc Agricola militum ardor eminebat, et finem orationis ingens alacritas consecuta est, statimque ad arma discursum. Instinctos ruentesque ita disposuit, ut peditum auxilia, quae octo milium erant, mediam aciem firmarent, equitum tria milia cornibus affunderentur. Legiones pro vallo stetere, ingens victoriae decus citra Romanum sanguinem bellandi, et auxilium, si pellerentur. Britannorum acies in speciem simul ac terrorem editioribus locis constiterat ita, ut primum agmen aequo, ceteri per acclive iugum connexi velut insurgerent; media campi covinnarius eques strepitu ac discursu complebat. Tum Agricola superante hostium multitudine veritus, ne in frontem simul et latera suorum pugnaretur, diductis ordinibus, quamquam porrectior acies futura erat, et arcessendas plerique legiones admonebant, promptior in spem et firmus adversis dimisso equo pedes ante vexilla constitit.

XXXVI. Ac primo congressu eminus certabatur, simulque constantia simul arte Britanni ingentibus

gladiis et brevibus cetris missilia nostrorum vitare vel
excutere, atque ipsi magnam vim telorum super-
fundere, donec Agricola Batavorum cohortes ac Tun-
grorum duas cohortatus est, ut rem ad mucrones ac
manus adducerent; quod et ipsis vetustate militiae
exercitatum et hostibus inhabile, parva scuta et enor-
mes gladios gerentibus. Nam Britannorum gladii
sine mucrone complexum armorum et in aperto pugnam
non tolerabant. Igitur ut Batavi miscere ictus, ferire
umbonibus, ora foedare, et stratis, qui in aequo astite-
rant, erigere in colles aciem coepere, ceterae cohortes
aemulatione et impetu connisae proximos quosque cae-
dere; ac plerique semineces aut integri festinatione
victoriae relinquebantur. Interim equitum turmae
fugere, covinnarii peditum se proelio miscuere, et
quamquam recentem terrorem intulerant, densis tamen hostium agminibus et inaequalibus locis hae-
rebant; minimeque equestris ea iam pugnae facies
erat, quum aegre clivo instantes simul equorum
corporibus impellerentur; ac saepe vagi currus, ex-
territi sine rectoribus equi, ut quemque formido
tulerat, transversos aut obvios incursabant.

XXXVII. Et Britanni, qui adhuc pugnae expertes summa collium insederant et paucitatem nostrorum vacui spernebant, degredi paulatim et circum-
ire terga vincentium coeperant, ni id ipsum veritus
Agricola quattuor equitum alas, ad subita belli
retentas, venientibus opposuisset, quantoque ferocius
accucurrerant, tanto acrius pulsos in fugam disiecisset.
Ita consilium Britannorum in ipsos versum, trans-
vectaeque praecepto ducis a fronte pugnantium alae
aversam hostium aciem invasere. Tum vero patentibus locis grande et atrox spectaculum; sequi, vulne-

rare, capere, atque eosdem, oblatis aliis, trucidare.
Iam hostium, prout cuique ingenium erat, catervae
armatorum paucioribus terga praestare, quidam inermes ultro ruere ac se morti offerre; passim arma
et corpora et laceri artus et cruenta humus, et aliquando etiam victis ira virtusque. Postquam silvis
appropinquaverunt, collecti primos sequentium, incau-
tos et locorum ignaros, circumveniebant. Quod ni
frequens ubique Agricola validas et expeditas cohortes
indaginis modo, et, sicubi artiora erant, partem equitum dimissis equis, simul rariores silvas equitem persultare iussisset, acceptum aliquod vulnus per nimiam
fiduciam foret. Ceterum ubi compositos firmis ordinibus sequi rursus videre, in fugam versi non agminibus, ut prius, nec alius alium respectantes; rari et
vitabundi invicem longinqua atque avia petiere. Finis
sequendi nox et satietas fuit. Caesa hostium ad decem
milia; nostrorum trecenti sexaginta cecidere, in quis
Aulus Atticus praefectus cohortis, iuvenili ardore et
ferocia equi hostibus illatus.

XXXVIII. Et nox quidem gaudio praedaque
laeta victoribus. Britanni palantes mixtoque virorum
mulierumque ploratu trahere vulneratos, vocare · in-
tegros, deserere domos ac per iram ultro incendere;
eligere latebras et statim relinquere, miscere invicem
consilia aliqua, deinde separare, aliquando frangi
aspectu pignorum suorum, saepius concitari; satisque
constabat saevisse quosdam in coniuges ac liberos,
tamquam misererentur. Proximus dies faciem victoriae
latius aperuit; vastum ubique silentium, secreti colles,
fumantia procul tecta, nemo exploratoribus obvius.
Quibus in omnem partem dimissis, ubi incerta fugae
vestigia neque usquam conglobari hostes compertum,

et exacta iam aestate spargi bellum nequibat, in fine,
Borestorum exercitum deducit.   Ibi acceptis obsidibus, praefecto classis circumvehi Britanniam prae-
cipit.   Datae ad id vires, et praecesserat terror.   Ipse
peditem atque equites lento itinere, quo novarum
gentium animi ipsa transitus mora terrerentur, in
hibernis locavit; et simul classis secunda tempestate
ac fama Trutulensem portum tenuit, unde proximo
Britanniae latere lecto omni redierat.

XXXIX.   Hunc rerum cursum, quamquam nulla
verborum iactantia epistolis Agricolae auctum, ut
Domitiano moris erat, fronte laetus, pectore anxius
excepit.   Inerat conscientia derisui fuisse nuper falsum
e Germania triumphum, emptis per commercia, quorum
habitus et crines in captivorum speciem formarentur;
at nunc veram magnamque victoriam tot milibus
hostium caesis ingenti fama celebrari.   Id sibi maxime
formidolosum, privati hominis nomen supra principis
attolli; frustra studia fori et civilium artium decus
in silentium acta, si militarem gloriam alius occuparet;
et cetera utcumque facilius dissimulari, ducis boni
imperatoriam virtutem esse.   Talibus curis exercitus,
quodque saevae cogitationis indicium erat, secreto suo
satiatus, optimum in praesentia statuit reponere odium,
donec impetus famae et favor exercitus languesceret.
Nam etiamtum Agricola Britanniam obtinebat.

XL.—XLVI. A.D. 84.—A.D. 93.   *Recall of Agricola.*
  His cold reception by the Emperor.   His grow-
  ing popularity and consequent danger from the
  Emperor's jealousy.   He declines a Proconsulate.
  His death; its suspicious circumstances; why oppor-
  tune and to be desired.   Concluding reflexions on
  Agricola.

XL. Igitur triumphalia ornamenta et illustris statuae honorem, et quicquid pro triumpho datur, multo verborum honore cumulata, decerni in senatu iubet, addique insuper opinionem Syriam provinciam Agricolae destinari, vacuam tum morte Atilii Rufi consularis et maioribus reservatam. Credidere plerique libertum ex secretioribus ministeriis missum ad Agricolam codicillos, quibus ei Syria dabatur, tulisse, cum praecepto, ut, si in Britannia foret, traderentur; eumque libertum in ipso freto oceani obvium Agricolae, ne appellato quidem eo ad Domitianum remeasse, sive verum istud, sive ex ingenio principis fictum ac compositum est. Tradiderat interim Agricola successori suo provinciam quietam tutamque. Ac ne notabilis celebritate et frequentia occurrentium introitus esset, vitato amicorum officio noctu in urbem, noctu in palatium, ita ut praeceptum erat, venit, exceptusque brevi osculo et nullo sermone turbae servientium immistus est. Ceterum, ut militare nomen, grave inter otiosos, aliis virtutibus temperaret, tranquillitatem atque otium penitus auxit, cultu modicus, sermone facilis, uno aut altero amicorum comitatus, adeo uti plerique, quibus magnos viros per ambitionem aestimare mos est, viso aspectoque Agricola quaererent famam, pauci interpretarentur.

XLI. Crebro per eos dies apud Domitianum absens accusatus, absens absolutus est. Causa periculi non crimen ullum aut querela laesi cuiusquam, sed infensus virtutibus princeps et gloria viri ac pessimum inimicorum genus, laudantes. Et ea insecuta sunt rei publicae tempora, quae sileri Agricolam non sinerent; tot exercitus in Moesia Daciaque et Germania et Pannonia temeritate aut per ignaviam du-

cum amissi, tot militares viri cum tot cohortibus expugnati et capti; nec iam de limite imperii et ripa,
sed de hibernis legionum et possessione dubitatum.
Ita cum damna damnis continuarentur, atque omnis
annus funeribus et cladibus insigniretur, poscebatur.
ore vulgi dux Agricola, comparantibus cunctis vi-
gorem et constantiam et expertum bellis animum
cum inertia et formidine ceterorum.   Quibus sermonibus satis constat Domitiani quoque aures verberatas, dum optimus quisque libertorum amore et
fide, pessimi malignitate et livore pronum deteriori-
bus principem exstimulabant. Sic Agricola simul suis
virtutibus, simul vitiis aliorum in ipsam gloriam
praeceps agebatur.

XLII.   Aderat iam annus, quo proconsulatum
Asiae et Africae sortiretur, et occiso Civica nuper
nec Agricolae consilium deerat nec Domitiano exemplum.   Accessere quidam cogitationum principis periti, qui iturusne esset in provinciam ultro Agricolam
interrogarent.   Ac primo occultius quietem et otium
laudare, mox operam suam in approbanda excusa-
tione offerre; postremo non iam obscuri suadentes
simul terrentesque pertraxere ad Domitianum.   Qui
paratus simulatione, in arrogantiam compositus et
audiit preces excusantis, et quum annuisset, agi
sibi gratias passus est, nec erubuit beneficii invidia.
Salarium tamen, proconsulari solitum offerri et qui-
busdam a se ipso concessum, Agricolae non dedit,
sive offensus non petitum, sive ex conscientia, ne,
quod vetuerat, videretur emisse.   Proprium humani
ingenii est odisse, quem laeseris; Domitiani vero
natura, praeceps in iram, et quo obscurior eo irrevocabilior, moderatione tamen prudentiaque Agricolae

leniebatur, quia non contumacia neque inani iacta-
tione libertatis famam fatumque provocabat. Sciant,
quibus moris est illicita mirari, posse etiam sub malis
principibus magnos viros esse, obsequiumque ac modestiam, si industria ac vigor assint, eo laudis excedere, quo plerique per abrupta, sed in nullum rei
publicae usum, ambitiosa morte inclaruerunt.

XLIII. Finis vitae eius nobis luctuosus, amicis
tristis, extraneis etiam ignotisque non sine cura fuit.
Vulgus quoque et hic aliud agens populus et ventita-
vere ad domum et per fora et circulos locuti sunt,
nec quisquam audita morte Agricolae aut laetatus est,
aut statim oblitus. Et augebat miserationem constans rumor veneno interceptum. Nobis nihil comperti affirmare ausim. Ceterum per omnem valetu-
dinem eius, crebrius quam ex more principatus per
nuntios visentis, et libertorum primi et medicorum
intimi venere, sive cura illud sive inquisitio erat.
Supremo quidem die momenta ipsa deficientis per
dispositos cursores nuntiata constabat, nullo credente
sic accelerari, quae tristis audiret. Speciem tamen
doloris animo vultuque prae se tulit, securus iam odii,
et qui facilius dissimularet gaudium quam metum.
Satis constabat lecto testamento Agricolae, quo coheredem optimae uxori et piissimae filiae Domitianum
scripsit, laetatum eum velut honore iudicioque. Tam
caeca et corrupta mens assiduis adulationibus erat, ut
nesciret a bono patre non scribi heredem nisi malum
principem.

XLIV. Natus erat Agricola Gaio Caesare tertium consule Idibus Iuniis; excessit quarto et quin-
quagesimo anno, decimo Kalendas Septembres Collega
Priscoque consulibus. Quod si habitum quoque eius

posteri noscere velint, decentior quam sublimior
fuit; nihil metus in vultu; gratia oris supercrat.
Bonum virum facile crederes, magnum libenter. Et
ipse quidem, quamquam medio in spatio integrae
aetatis ereptus, quantum ad gloriam, longissimum
aevum peregit; quippe et vera bona, quae in virtutibus sita sunt, impleverat, et consulari ac triumphalibus ornamentis praedito quid aliud astruere fortuna
poterat? Opibus nimiis non gaudebat, speciosae con
tigerant. Filia atque uxore superstitibus potest videri etiam beatus incolumi dignitate, florente fama,
salvis affinitatibus et amicitiis, futura effugisse. Nam
sicuti durare in hanc beatissimi seculi lucem ac principem Traianum videre quondam augurio votisque
apud nostras aures ominabatur, ita festinatae mortis
grande solatium tulit evasisse postremum illud tempus, quo Domitianus non iam per intervalla ac spira-
menta temporum, sed continuo et velut uno ictu rem
publicam exhausit.

XLV. Non vidit Agricola obsessam curiam et
clausum armis senatum, et eadem strage tot consularium caedes, tot nobilissimarum feminarum exilia et
fugas. Una adhuc victoria Carus Metius censebatur,
et intra Albanam arcem sententia Messalini strepebat,
et Massa Baebius tum reus erat. Mox nostrae duxere
Helvidium in carcerem manus, nos Maurici Rusticique
visus, nos innocenti sanguine Senecio perfudit. Nero
tamen subtraxit oculos suos, iussitque scelera, non
spectavit; praecipua sub Domitiano miseriarum pars
erat videre et aspici, quum suspiria nostra subscriberentur, quum denotandis tot hominum palloribus
sufficeret saevus ille vultus et rubor, quo se contra
pudorem muniebat.

Tū vero felix, Agricola, nōn vītae tantum clāritāte, sed etiam opportūnitāte mortis. Ut perhibent, qui interfuerunt novissimis sermonibus tuis, constans et libens fatum excepisti, tamquam pro virili portione innocentiam principi donares. ‘ Sed mihi filiaeque eius praeter acerbitatem parentis erepti auget maestitiam, quod assidere valetudini, fovere deficientem, satiari vultu complexuque non contigit. Excepissemus certe mandata vocesque, quas penitus animo figeremus. Noster hic dolor, nostrum vulnus ; nobis tum longae absentiae condicione ante quadriennium amissus est. Omnia sine dubio, optime parentum, assidente amantissima uxore superfuere honori tuo ; paucioribus tamen lacrimis compositus es, et novissima in luce desideravere aliquid oculi tui.

XLVI. Si quis piorum manibus locus, si, ut sapientibus placet, non cum corpore extinguuntur magnae animae, placide quiescas, nosque, domum tuam, ab infirmo desiderio et mulicbribus lamentis ad contemplationem virtutum tuarum voces, quas neque lugeri neque plangi fas est. Admiratione te potius quam temporalibus laudibus, et, si natura suppeditet, aemulatione decoremus. Is verus honos, ea coniunctissimi cuiusque pietas. Id filiae quoque uxorique praeceperim, sic patris, sic mariti memoriam venerari, ut omnia facta dictaque eius secum revolvant, formamque ac figuram animi magis quam corporis complectantur ; non quia intercedendum putem imaginibus, quae marmore aut aere finguntur ; sed ut vultus hominum, ita simulacra vultus imbecilla ac mortalia sunt, forma mentis aeterna, quam tenere et exprimere non per alienam materiam et artem, sed tuis ipse moribus possis. Quicquid ex Agricola amavimus, quicquid mirati sumus, manet mansurumque est in animis hominum, in aeternitate temporum, fama rerum.   Nam multos veterum velut inglorios et ignobiles oblivio obruit ; Agricola posteritati narratus et traditus superstes erit.

NOTES.

CHAPTER I.

1. **Antiquitus usitatum.**] *Usitatum* is in attribution to the noun-infinitive tradere, tradere being the object of the verb omisit.

2. **Quamquam.**] The word is commonly used to introduce a distinct clause; 'quamvis' is generally employed to qualify a single word.

3. **Incuriosa suorum.**] 'Neglectful of its own sons,' not 'glories.' Comp. *Ann.* II. 88, vetera extollimus, recentium *incuriosi;* also Hor. *C.* III. 24, 31—2, virtutem incolumem, odimus, sublatam ex oculis quaerimus *invidi.*

4. **Supergressa est.**] 'Has risen superior to;' has past into a region which invidia cannot reach. Comp. *Ann.* XIV. 54, invidia *infra* tuam magnitudinem jacet.

5. **Ignorantiam recti et invidiam.**] 'Blindness and hostility to goodness' (*C* and *B*). It is very doubtful, however, whether invidiam is to be connected with recti. The expression 'invidia recti' would scarcely be allowable. The rectum (right) which the multitude are incapable of discerning is not exactly the aspect of virtue against which invidia is felt. And yet the presence of the singular vitium in the preceding clause compels us to join the two phrases. Rectum is equivalent here to virtus. Comp. *Hist.* III. 51, exempla *recti*, and IV. 5, *recti* pervicax.

6. **Pronum magisque in aperto.**] 'Pronum' expresses the inclination of the will; 'in aperto' the favouring circumstances. Or we may take both phrases as referring to the circumstances; the path to virtue was pronus, sc. not arduus, and in aperto, sc. not impeditus.

7. **Sine gratia aut ambitione.**] 'Without partiality or self-seeking.' 'Gratia' expresses the bias felt by a writer possibly towards unworthy persons; 'ambitio' the unprincipled desire for advancement which would betray him into flattery.

3—2

8. Conscientiae.] Comp. the use of the word in ch. 2, *conscientiam* generis humani, and 42, sive ex *conscientia*, ne quod vetuerat videretur emisse. 'Bonae *conscientiae* pretium' is the feeling that they had acted rightly.

9. Ipsi.] 'Ipsorum' would be more strictly grammatical, but would clash unpleasantly with 'morum' later on in the sentence. The nominative 'ipsi' is borrowed from what would be the equivalent conditional clause, 'Si suam ipsi vitam narrarent.' Comp. Sallust, *Jug.* 18, exercitus, amisso duce, ac passim *multis sibi quisque* imperium *petentibus*, brevi dilabitur.

10. Citra fidem.] That which falls short of (citra) or goes beyond (ultra) belief (fides) does not meet with credit. Comp. *Germ.* 16, *citra* speciem=falling short of beauty. For the subject of autobiography generally comp. Cic. *Epist. ad Fam.* v. 12, where the writer says that if his friend Lucceius cannot write about him, he must write about himself, and would have good precedents in doing so, and continues thus: Sed quod te non fugit, haec sunt in hoc genere vitia; et verecundius ipsi de sese scribant necesse est si quid est laudandum, et praetereant si quid reprehendendum est. Accedit etiam ut minor sit fides, minor auctoritas, etc.

11. At nunc narraturo...tempora.] Comp. *Hist.* I. 1, Ambitionem scriptoris facile averseris, livor et detrectatio pronis auribus accipiuntur. Tacitus feels that he might rely on the acceptance which satire and invective always meet with, and need not, had these, and not praise, been his theme, have asked for indulgence. The use of the perfect 'fuit' may be best expressed by such a paraphrase as 'Before I begin to relate I have found it necessary, etc.' The 'tempora' are the times of Domitian. For 'incusaturus' Ritter reads 'incursaturus.' He refers the 'nunc' to Domitian's days, makes 'venia' equivalent to 'leave,' and supposes 'incursaturus' to mean 'likely to offend.' Tacitus thus is made to say that he would not have asked for a permission which would have been likely to offend a *régime* (tempora) that was hostile to virtue. 'Fuit' would then be equivalent to 'fuisset.' For the expression 'infesta virtutibus' comp. Cic. *Orat. ad Brut.* 10. Hoc sum aggressus, statim Catone absoluto, quem nunquam attigissem, tempora timens *inimica virtuti;* a curious parallel to the sentiment of this chapter.

CHAPTER II.

1. Legimus.] Most probably this means 'we read,' or 'it is recorded in history.' But it may be opposed to 'vidimus,' and imply that Tacitus was himself absent and heard only of these occurrences. Kritz refers it to the *Acta Diurna*, and would understand by it, 'it was positively recorded (so evil were the

NOTES. 37

times) in official documents' (as we might say in the *Gazette*). This seems a far-fetched explanation, and the passage which he quotes from Dion Cassius (LXVII. 11) tells against it, as it states that in his later years Domitian forbad the names of his victims to be inscribed in the *acta*.

2. **Triumviris.**] These were the 'triumviri capitales,' who combined some of the duties of our police magistrates and our sheriffs.

3. **Comitio ac foro.**] The comitium was part of the forum. A certain solemnity is given to the sentence by the use of the two words. Comp. the use of Romani Quirites.

4. **Scilicet.**] The word is used ironically. 'They fancied, forsooth.'

5. **Conscientiam.**] 'The approving knowledge.' It was hoped that, all records of these actions being destroyed, mankind could never express its approval of them. This is a step towards the meaning which our word 'conscience' has now reached.

6. **Arbitrabantur.**] Sc. Domitian and his satellites.

7. **Expulsis insuper, &c.**] Comp. Plin. *Epp.* III. 11, quum essent *philosophi ab urbe summoti.*

8. **Omni bona arte, &c.**] Comp. Plin. *Panegyr.* 47, quum sibi vitiorum omnium conscius princeps inimicas vitiis artes non odio magis quam reverentia relegaret.

9. **Ultimum.**] Sc. the last point that could be reached, 'the extreme.'

10. **Adempto per inquisitiones, &c.**] By 'inquisitiones' is meant the espionage of the informer, which made men afraid either to speak their own thoughts or to listen to the thoughts of others.

CHAPTER III.

1. **Nerva Caesar.**] This passage marks the date of this work, or, at least, of these prefatory chapters, as being between the adoption of Trajan by Nerva (whence the name *Nerva* Trajanus) and Nerva's death. In *Hist.* I. 1, we read of Divus Nerva. Nerva adopted Trajan towards the end of A.D. 97, and died Jan. 27 in the following year.

2. **Principatum.**] 'Principatus' is the form of government which puts a 'Princeps' (in the case of Rome it was a 'Princeps Senatus') at the head of the state. Comp. *Hist.* I. 1, *principatum* Divi Nervae, where, as here, there may be some allusion to the specially *civil* character of Nerva's rule.

3. **Temporum.**] This is the reading of the MSS., which Ritter alters into *imperii*, in order to complete the parallel between this and the passage quoted above, in which we have *imperium* Trajani. Comp. however, *Hist.* I. 1, *rara temporum* felicitate.

4. **Securitas publica.**] The personified Fortune of the state. The figure of a goddess bearing this name is found on coins of the Antonine period.

5. **Nec spem modo ac votum, etc.**] 'Has not only *our* hopes and good wishes' *'C* and *B).* This rendering has the advantage of giving a meaning to 'assumpserit,' which comprehends both of its objects 'spem ac votum,' and 'ipsius voti fiduciam et robur.' But the hopes and good wishes may be those of the 'Securitas publica' for herself. We must then supply out of 'assumpserit' some such notion as 'conceperit,' and render 'has only conceived hopes, &c. but secured' ('assumpserit') &c.

6. **Ipsius voti.**] 'Of the wish itself,' *i. e.* of the thing wished for, *fiduciam et robur,* possibly an hendiadys for 'strong assurance;' or it may be rendered 'the certainty and substance.'

7. **Robur.**] 'Substance.' It is used somewhat similarly for 'the heart' or 'the best part,' as in '*robur* militum.' Cic. *Epist. ad Fam.* X. 33.

8. **Ingenia studiaque.**] 'Genius and its pursuits' (*C* and *B*).

9. **Quindecim annos.**] The fifteen years of Domitian's reign, A.D. 81—96.

10. **Quid, si...non tamen.**] The connection is 'in spite of these losses, the removal of our best men, and the injury suffered by ourselves, yet we shall not regret to have told, &c.'

11. **Promptissimus quisque.**] 'The most energetic,' 'the most ready (promptus) for what had to be done.' Comp. Sall. *Cat.* 7, ingenium *in promptu* habet.

12. **Nostri superstites.**] Sc. surviving our own powers. The meaning is, 'only a few of us are left, and we are not what we were.'

13. **Juvenes ad senectutem.**] Tacitus includes himself in this class. See on this subject his Life prefixed to this edition.

14. **Servitutis.**] An obvious correction of the reading of the MSS. which is 'senectutis.'

15. **Non tamen pigebit, etc.**] This must be taken to refer to the *Historiae,* on which Tacitus was already engaged.

16. **Interim.]** 'Meanwhile,' *i. e.* till the more important work is executed.

17. **Honori Agricolae, &c.]** The writer's is not now, so to speak, a political object, but it is to do honour to a good man. He thus returns to the subject announced in the first chapter.

18. **Professione pietatis.]** Sc. on the strength of its shewing filial regard.'

CHAPTER IV.

1. **Forojuliensium colonia.]** Now Fréjus, about 25 miles S.W. of Nice. It was named after its founder C. Julius Caesar.

2. **Caesaris.]** This reading seems preferable to 'Caesarum.' Both grandfathers were probably Procurators under Augustus, the father having been made a Senator by Tiberius.

3. **Quae equestris nobilitas est.]** There is some difficulty about these words. Wex considers them to be spurious on the ground that really distinguished equites, such as are called primores equitum (*Hist.* I. 4) and equites dignitate senatoria (*Ann.* XVI. 17), looked down upon the office of Procurator. In support of this view he quotes the latter passage which seems to imply that Mela, who was an eques dignitate Senatoria, was thought to have acted strangely when he accepted a Procuratorship for the sake of making a speedy fortune. Kritz, on the other hand, affirms that the office was bestowed *only* on the more distinguished members of the equestrian order. If the words are genuine they must mean that the circumstance of having one or both grandfathers a Procurator constituted equestrian nobility. The term 'nobilis' was opposed to 'novus homo,' and meant strictly a man whose father or ancestor had risen to a curule magistracy. The dignity of a Procuratorship would constitute a corresponding 'nobilitas' among the equites.

4. **Fuit.]** This is the conjecture for 'Julii,' the reading of the MSS.

5. **Meritus.]** 'Earned.' There is an irony in the expression very characteristic of Tacitus.

6. **In hujus sinu...educatur.]** 'Brought up by her side with fond affection' (*C* and *B*); 'in sinu' means that his mother's personal care was bestowed upon him. Comp. *Dial. de Orat.* 28, filius, ex casta parente natus, non in cella emptae nutricis sed *gremio ac sinu matris* educabatur. The strictly classical usage of 'indulgentia' is in its favourable sense, but Quintilian I. 2 employs it in the other, 'mollis illa educatio quam *indulgentiam* vocamus.'

7. **Peccantium.**] 'Peccare' denotes here 'sins of licen-tiousness,' as commonly in the Roman poets; comp. Hor. *C.* III. xix. 20, *peccare docentes historias.*

8. **Sedem ac magistram.**] 'The scene and guide' (*C* and *B*). The place is said, as, by a common metaphor, Oxford or Cam-bridge might be said, to have guided his studies.

9. **Locum...compositum.**] The 'comitas' (courtesy or refinement) prevented the rudeness which might have attached otherwise to the 'parsimonia.' For 'parsimonia' comp. *Ann.* III. 55, ·novi homines, e municipiis et coloniis atque etiam provinciis in senatum adsumpti, *domesticam parsimoniam* intulerunt. For the character of Massilia comp. Cic. *pro Flacco,* 26, neque te, Massilia, praetereo..... Cujus ego civitatis disciplinam non solum Graeciae sed haud scio an cunctis gentibus anteponendam jure dicam, etc., and *Ann.* IV. 44, where we are told that Augustus banished Lucius Antonius to Massilia, ubi specie studiorum nomen exilii tegeretur.

10. **Acrius hausisse.**] The meaning seems to be that Agricola had conceived and would have continued to indulge this passion, had not his mother checked it. Comp. for the elliptical construction, ch. 37, Britanni degredi...*coeperant, ni* Agricola quatuor equitum alas venientibus opposuisset; *i. e.* the Britons had begun to descend *and would have continued to do so* had not Agricola so acted. Orelli takes 'acrius' as an adjective agreeing with 'studium.' Perhaps it is better to consider it an adverb qualifying 'hausisse.'

11. **Prudentia matris.**] Comp. Suet. *Nero,* 52, a philo-sophia eum mater avertit monens imperaturo contrariam esse.

12. **Scilicet.**] 'It was the case of.'

13. **Speciem.**] Species may have its common meaning of 'beauty;' or it may have its philosophical sense of 'ideal' (ἰδέα), as in Cic. *Orat. ad Brut.* 5, insidebat in ejus mente *species* elo-quentiae, quam cernebat animo, re ipsa non videbat.

14. **Vehementius quam caute.**] The classical usage would be 'vehementius quam cautius.' Tacitus generally follows this, but sometimes has that of the text, as *Hist.* I. 83, Tumultus proximi initium pietas vestra *acrius quam considerate* excitavit.

15. **Mox mitigavit......aetas.**] '(Maturer) reason and (advancing) age mellowed his temper.'

16. **Modum.**] Aristotle's τὸ μέσον. Comp. Hor. *Sat.* I. i. 106, Est *modus* in rebus, and *Ep.* I. vi. 15, Insani sapiens nomen ferat, aequus iniqui, Ultra quam satis est virtutem si petat ipsam.

CHAPTER V.

1. **Prima castrorum rudimenta.**] 'His military apprenticeship' (*C* and *B*). 'Castra' is used for 'military service,' as in ch. 16, nullis *castrorum* experimentis.

2. **Approbavit.**] Sc. so served as to satisfy.

3. **Suetonio Paullino.**] For Tacitus' opinion of this general comp. *Hist.* II. 25, cunctator natura, &c., and II. 31, nemo illa tempestate rei militaris callidior habebatur.

4. **Contubernio aestimaret.**] 'Contubernio aestimare' is to form a judgment of character by the opportunities of close companionship. The practice may be compared to the relation in which in our service an aide-de-camp stands to his general officer. Comp. Sall. *Jug.* 64, in *contubernio* patris militabat, *Hist.* I. 23, *contubernales* appellando, where Otho wishes to make his military audience feel that there is a tie of intimacy between himself and them.

5. **Neque Agricola......rettulit.**] The general meaning is, that Agricola did not use the facilities afforded by his rank either to procure enjoyment or escape from duty. His rank (titulus) with one disposed to indulgence (expressed by licenter) would have given opportunities for pleasure (voluptates). On the other hand, had he been idly disposed (expressed by segniter), his inexperience (inscitia), *i. e.* the fact that he was of little use, would have made it easy to get leave of absence (commeatus). 'Rettulit' may be rendered by 'employed with a view to,' &c.; 'referre ad aliquid' being equivalent to our expression 'to refer to an end;' comp. Plin. *Epp.* I. 22, nihil ad ostentationem, omnia ad conscientiam *refert*. For 'commeatus' comp. *Ann.* XV. 10, reliquas legiones promiscuis *commeatibus* infirmaverat.

6. **Nihil appetere in jactationem.**] 'To attempt nothing for display' (*C* and *B*); or more exactly, perhaps, 'to seek for no service with a view to display;' 'appetere' being opposed to 'recusare.'

7. **Anxius et intentus.**] 'Careful and vigilant' (*C* and *B*); or 'careful and energetic.' He was full of thought before the time of action, and when the time was come wholly occupied with what he was doing. 'Intentus' gives the idea of the full tension of energy.

8. **Excitatior.**] This is the conjecture of Buchner, which we have followed Kritz in adopting instead of 'exercitatior.' It means 'more excited,' and would seem the natural expression of Tacitus in speaking of the native tribes; *exercitatior* would apply rather to the Roman province.

9. **Trucidati veterani.**] Comp. ch. 16, where Boadicea's attack on Camalodunum is described. Some veterans appear to have been settled in this colony. It was, in fact, the only real *colonia* in Britain, but the word is used loosely of important towns; comp. note on *aegra municipia*, ch. 32.

10. **Intersepti.**] Armies would be said to be 'intersepti' when they were prevented from joining the main body; comp. *Hist.* III. 53, *Intersepta* Germanorum Rhaetorumque auxilia. We have followed the reading of the MSS. though perhaps *intercepti*, 'cut off' or 'surprised,' gives a sense agreeing better with the description of the revolt.

11. **Cessit in ducem.**] 'Fell to the share of the general.'

12. **Temporibus.**] It is best to take this as a dative depending on ingrata. Kritz considers it to be an ablative, though he quotes ch. 31, 'virtus subjectorum *ingrata imperantibus.*'

13. **Quibus sinistra...interpretatio.**] Kritz would supply 'ejus,' *i. e.* 'militaris gloriae,' and render in which there is, in the case of eminent men, a sinister interpretation put on military glory. This seems far-fetched and disproved by the position of 'sinistra.' It is better to join the word to 'erga eminentes.'

CHAPTER VI.

1. **Hinc.**] Sc. 'from or after these services.'

2. **Natalibus.**] 'Lineage,' a post-Augustan use of the word.

3. **Decus.**] 'Distinction.' The word here means the reflected lustre that comes to a man from great connections.

4. **Per mutuam caritatem.**] Orelli takes 'per' to signify time, as if 'in continuous mutual affection' was meant. It seems better to take it as causal. Their affection was the cause of their singular harmony.

5. **Nisi quod......laus.**] 'However, the good wife deserves the greater praise' (*C* and *B*). 'Nisi quod' is Tacitus' comment on the praise which he has been bestowing on Agricola in the previous sentence. He guards himself from being supposed to say that the husband and wife deserve equal commendation. In his view the good wife deserves more.

6. **Sors Quaesturae.**] The Quaestors were appointed, and *then* drew lots for their destinations.

7. **Salvius Titianus.**] He was the elder brother of M. Otho, afterwards Emperor. Comp. *Hist.* I. 75, 77.

8. **Mutuam dissimulationem.**] ' A mutual concealment of guilt' (*C* and *B*). Comp. *Hist.* I. 72, *vices impunitatis*, and Plin. *Epp.* IX. 13, Senatus severus in ceteros senatoribus solis *dissimulatione quasi mutua* parceret.

9. **Subsidium.**] This possibly refers to the advantage which a candidate derived from having children. Comp. *Ann.* II. 51, plerique nitebantur ut *numerus liberorum in candidatis praepolleret.* This would be to carry out the provisions of the lex Papia Poppaea. We prefer to give it a more general signification.

10. **Sublatum.**] 'Born,' a phrase derived from the custom by which a Roman father took up (sustulit) the child whom he acknowledged, and wished to rear.

11. **Brevi amisit.**] This does not necessarily mean what Ritter understands by it, that the son died before the daughter was born. In that case we should rather have expected ' amiserat.' The daughter was a 'subsidium,' as increasing his family, and when he lost his son became a 'solatium.'

12. **Quibus inertia......fuit.**] Comp. Tacitus' account of Galba, *Hist.* I. 49, metus temporum obtentui fuit, ut quod *segnitia erat sapientia* vocaretur. In Agricola's case the 'segnitia' was of course assumed.

13. **Tenor et silentium.**] ' Consistent quietude' (*C* and *B*); ' tenor' is the correction of the MS. reading ' certior.'

14. **Neque enim jurisdictio obvenerat.**] There were twelve or more praetors, two of whom only, the praetor urbanus and the praetor peregrinus, had judicial functions. Agricola did not happen to hold either office.

15. **Ludos et inania honoris...duxit.**] 'The games and the pageantry of his office he ordered according to the mean' (*C* and *B*). It is possible that 'ducere' may be equivalent to 'edere,' with special reference to the procession, the notion of which would be included in the word 'ludi,' and which would be expressed by the phrase '*ducere* pompam.' It seems better, however, to connect 'duxit' closely with 'medio,' as if Tacitus meant to say 'he conducted them along the middle course.' Ritter considers it to be equivalent to 'arbitratus est,' but to make out this view he has to adopt the violent course of substituting for ' medio rationis' Lipsius' conjecture of moderationis.

16. **Famae propior.**] Sc. rather gaining distinction from them than otherwise. Though the exhibition was not prodigally ostentatious, there was enough splendour about it to attract admiration. Tacitus, it will be remembered, was himself praetor, and in that capacity presided over the Ludi Saeculares exhibited by Domitian, A.D. 88. See *Ann.* XI. 11, where he mentions this of himself.

17. **Electus a Galba.**] For an account of a similar measure of Galba's comp. *Hist.* I. 20, where we hear of the appointment of commissioners charged with the duty of recovering some of the prodigal bounties of Nero.

18. **Sensisset.**] The force of the pluperfect may be thus explained. He so ordered things that when his office was discharged it might be said that the State had received no injury (or, it may mean, had contracted no guilt), except from the irremediable wrongs which Nero had inflicted. Comp. Plin. *Paneg.* 40, 'Idem effecisti ne malos principes *habuissemus.*' Under Trajan's rule the evils of former misrule had ceased to exist. By a bold figure Rome—so entirely had she recovered—might be said, not even to have had bad Emperors.

CHAPTER VII.

1. **Nam classis Othoniana, etc.**] For the account of these events see *Hist.* II. 12, 13. Tacitus would probably have heard the details which he there gives from his father-in-law.

2. **Licenter.**] 'For purposes of plunder.'

3. **Intemelios.**] Now Vintimiglia, about twelve miles E. of Monaco.

4. **Quae causa caedis fuerat.**] We should rather expect 'quod.' But the meaning is that whatever of her moveable inherited property she had on the spot was plundered, and that it was this that had invited the crime.

5. **Solemnia pietatis.**] 'The solemn duties of filial affection.' The funeral would have been performed hastily, but some of the ceremonies could be repeated with more solemnity. Comp. Cic. *pro Cluent.* 9, where we are told of a mother, who finding that her son was dead, and his corpse already burnt, repeated the funeral rites (de integro funus jam sepulto filio fecit).

6. **Affectati a Vespasiano imperii.**] This event took place in the beginning of July, A.D. 69; see *Hist.* II. 79.

7. **Deprehensus.**] 'Overtaken.'

Mucianus.] Comp. *Hist.* IV. 11, 'Mucianus urbem ingressus cuncta simul in se traxit.' For the character of Vespasian's chief lieutenant see *Hist.* II. 5.

8. **Ex paterna fortuna, etc.**] 'From his father's elevation seeking merely to practise (usurpare) licentiousness.' Comp. *Hist.* IV. 2, 'stupris et adulteriis filium Principis agebat.'

9. **Juvene admodum Demitiano.**] Comp. *Hist.* III. 70, where Flavius Sabinus speaks of him as filium Vespasiani *vix puberem.* He was in his eighteenth year.

10. **Vicesimae legioni.**] This was one of the legions stationed in Britain. Comp. *Hist.* I. 60. For the feeling of the troops about Vespasian, comp. *Hist.* III. 44.

11. **Decessor.**] Sc. Roscius Coelius.

12. **Legatis consularibus.**] These were the chief officers of the province. Each legion had its own legatus *praetorius.*

13. **Nimia.**] 'Too strong.' Comp. Vell. *Paterc.* II. 32, 'esse Cn. Pompeium *nimium* jam liberae reipublicae.'

14. **Successor simul et ultor.**] For a similar conjunction of words comp. *Hist.* I. 40, scelus, cujus *ultor est quisquis successit.*

CHAPTER VIII.

1. **Vettius Bolanus.**] Compare his character as described in ch. 26.

2. **Feroci provincia dignum est.**] The present 'est' is used either because the statement is meant to apply to any province, or because Britain still at the time of writing merited the same epithet. 'Esset' and 'erat' have been conjectured. For the epithet 'ferox' (high-spirited) comp. ch. 11, plus *ferociae* Britanni praeferunt.

3. **Vim.**] 'Energy,' rather than 'military strength,' as Kritz makes it to be.

4. **Ne incresceret.**] 'That he might not grow too great.'

5. **Consularem.**] Sc. 'legatum.'

6. **Ex eventu.**] On the strength of the result.

7. **In suam famam.**] 'With a view to his own fame.' Comp. ch. 5, 'nihil appetere *in jactationem.*'

8. **Ad auctorem et ducem.**] The meaning of 'auctor' is illustrated in *Germ.* 14, where a chieftain's comrades are said sua fortia facta gloriae ejus assignare.

9. **Extra invidiam.**] Like the Greek expression ἐκτὸς πόδ᾽ ἔχειν. Comp. *Hist.* I. 49, 'Galbae medium ingenium, magis *extra vitia* quam cum virtutibus.'

CHAPTER IX.

1. **Revertentem.**] 'As he was returning.' It is possible that he did not return to Rome, but stopped on the way at his command in Aquitania.

2. **Inter patricios ascivit.**] Comp. for the phrase *Ann.* XI. 25, 'Iisdem diebus *in numerum patriciorum ascivit* Caesar vetustissimum quemque e senatu, etc.' The passage is worthy of note as showing the exhaustion, indicated by the new names which we meet with in Tacitus, of the old and even of the more recent Roman aristocracy.

3. **Splendidae dignitatis.**] A genitive of *quality.* For a similar construction comp. in this chapter, *egregiae spei* filiam.

4. **Administratione.**] 'From the importance of its duties.'

5. **Spe consulatus.**] Galba had passed in like manner from the government of Aquitania to the consulship. Comp. Suet. *Galba,* 6.

6. **Subtilitatem.**] Sc. the faculty of drawing nice distinctions.

7. **Secura.**] 'Summary,' sc. that has not the fear of appeals before it. 'Obtusior,' 'somewhat blunt,' sc. careless of refinements, aiming at practical rather than theoretical justice.

8. **Calliditatem.**] The word is here used in a bad sense, as Cic. *De Off.* I. 19, 'Scientia quae est remota a justitia *calliditas* potius quam sapientia est appellanda.'

9. **Quamvis inter togatos.**] That is, though acting as a judge among civilians, who would be keen to detect faults and possibly prejudiced. For this use of togatos comp. *Hist.* II. 20, *togatos* adloqueretur.

10. **Jam vero.**] 'And besides;' comp. ch. 21, *Jam vero* principum filios erudire.

11. **Divisa.**] 'Were kept distinct.' Comp. for the use of the words 'curæ,' 'remissiones,' in contrast *Dial. de Orat.* 28, ac non studia modo *curasque,* sed *remissiones* etiam.

12 **Conventus.**] 'Days of session,' when the more important trials would be taken.

13. **Persona.**] An affectation ; a character artificially kept up as on the stage.

14. **Tristitiam...exuerat.**] 'He was altogether without.' Comp. *Ann.* VI. 25, Agrippina feminarum vitia *exuerat.* 'Avaritia must mean something that might coexist with the integritas and abstinentia spoken of below ; as, e.g. an excess in strictness about the revenue, the fault of Galba, who is said to have been publicae pecuniae *avarus.*

15. **Referre.**] 'To mention ;' comp. *Hist.* I. 30, neque enim *relatu* virtutum in comparatione Othonis opus est.

16.   **Cui saepe etiam boni indulgent.**] Comp. *Hist.*
IV. 16, quando etiam *sapientibus cupido gloriae novissima exuitur,*
and Milton, Lycidas.

Fame ....
The last infirmity of noble mind.

The sentiment seems to have been a current one among the Stoics
and due originally to Plato.

17.   **Collegas.**]   Sc. those in command of neighbouring
provinces.

18.   **Procuratoribus.**]   Either in other provinces or in his
own. With these officers, as having special charge of the revenue,
the legate might easily come into collision.

19.   **Atteri.**]   'To get the worst of it,' 'to suffer some
damage.'

20.   **Minus triennium.**]   From three to five years was the
ordinary duration of a governor's term of office.   Comp. Dio
Cass. LII, καὶ ἀρχέτωσαν μήτε ἔλαττον ἐτῶν τριῶν (εἰ μή τις ἀδική-
σειέ τι) μὴ πλεῖον πέντε.

21.   **Statim ad spem.**]   Statim conveys the idea that the
expectation was immediate ; grammatically it is joined to 'revocatus.'

22.   **Dari.**]   'Was being offered to him;' sc. that it was
understood that he was to have it after his consulship.

23.   **Elegit.**]   The meaning is that sometimes common
report causes a man to be chosen, secures his selection.

24.   **Tum.**]   Ritter alters the word to *jam,* quite unneces-
sarily. 'Tum,' he thinks, would imply that the spes was not
fulfilled. But it may well mean 'even then.'

CHAPTER X.

1.   **Multis scriptoribus.**]   A Dative ; as in ch. 2, quum
Aruleno Rustico, *etc.* Of these writers Caesar, Livy, and the
elder Pliny would be the chief.

2.   **In comparationem, etc.**]   'To challenge a comparison.'

3.   **Perdomita est.**]   Comp. *Hist.* I. 2, Britannia *perdomita*
et statim missa.

4.   **Ita quae, etc.**]   'So it follows that what those who
wrote before this time (*priores*) embellished, &c.'

5.   **Rerum fide.**]   On the evidence of facts.

6. **Romana notitia.**] ' Roman geography.'

7. **Spatio ac coelo, etc.**] 'Spatium' means 'extent,' ' coelum,' 'geographical position,' as astronomically and scientifically determined. There is a reference to the division of the earth into zones. It seems that Tacitus (in common with other writers) believed both Spain and Germany to extend much further to the north than they actually do. On this supposition his meaning in this sentence would be that Britain lies opposite to Spain on the west, to Germany on the east, and to Gaul on the south ; but that in the two former cases the distance is so considerable that the fact has to be inferred from certain considerations (expressed by the words spatio ac coelo), whereas in the case of Gaul it was a matter of ocular demonstration, Gallis etiam inspicitur. It will be remembered that Tacitus included Scandinavia in what he called Germany.

8. **Nullis contra terris.**] Comp. Caesar, *B. G.* II. 14, Tertium latus est contra septemtrionem, cui parti *nulla est objecta terra.*

9. **Oblongae scutulae, etc.**] It is not easy to see what conception Tacitus had formed of the shape of Britain. He seems to have shared the passion for discovering resemblances common to the ancient geographers. It has been doubted whether *scutula* means a 'dish,' or a mathematical figure ; and, taking the later supposition, whether it signifies a rhombus, a rhomboid, or a trapezium. We incline to the latter opinion, and may imagine the southern shore to be the longest side of the trapezium. The opposite or northern boundary would be the shortest. This figure would bear some resemblance to the bipennis, if we suppose the *iron head only* of that weapon to be intended. But from this northern boundary, which one might have supposed to be the extreme limit of the country (*extremo* jam littore) there extended a vast projection, narrowing in a wedge-like shape (in cuneum). Excluding Caledonia (citra Caledoniam) the country was like a *scutula* or *bipennis.*

10. **In universum fama est transgressa.**] The MSS. favour the reading 'in universum,' which the sense seems to demand. Because this resemblance is real as to part of the island, it has been supposed to be so about the whole. 'Universis,' which Orelli reads, and which he interprets in this way, can hardly bear such a meaning. Kritz reads 'transgressis,' which he takes to mean 'among those who have crossed over [from the continent into Britain].' This strikes us as a very questionable rendering.

11. **Hanc oram.**] i.e. the wedge-like projection of northern Britain.

12. **Novissimi maris.**] The furthest sea. Comp. *Hist.* v.

2, *novissima* Libyae, sc. the farthest part of Africa towards the East.

13. **Dispecta.**] 'Seen from a distance.'

14. **Thule.**] Probably not Iceland, but Mainland, the chief of the Shetlands.

15. **Hactenus jussum.**] 'Their orders were to go so far [and no further].'

16. **Minus appetebat.**] 'Was approaching,' a frequent use of the word. We have followed the reading of Kritz who corrects the statement of Orelli about the MSS.

17. **Ne ventis quidem perinde attolli.**] 'Not *even* raised by the winds as much as other seas.'

18. **Continui maris.**] 'Sea unbroken by land.'

19. **Fluminum.**] These 'flumina' are currents of the sea, locally called 'races.'

20. **Ferre.**] The word is here used absolutely; comp. Caesar, *B. G.* III. 15, quo ventus *ferebat.*

21. **Accrescere ac resorberi.**] 'Flow and ebb.'

22. **Littore tenus.**] 'Up to the shore and no further.'

23. **Penitus.**] 'Far inland.'

24. **Inseri.**] Used in a middle sense, 'makes its way.'

CHAPTER XI.

1. **Ut inter barbaros.**] 'As might be expected among barbarians.'

2. **Parum compertum.**] Comp. ch. 10, nondum *comperta.*

3. **Habitus corporum.**] Comp. *Germ.* 4, *habitus corporum* ...idem, and ch. 5, *corporibus habitum* dedit. It may be rendered 'physical characteristics.'

4. **Ex eo.**] Sc. from the fact that they are various.

5. **Rutilae Caledoniam, etc.**] Comp. *Germ.* 4, [Germanorum] *rutilae comae, magna corpora.*

6. **Colorati.**] 'Dark-coloured,' 'sun-burnt.'

7. **Torti.**] 'Curly.'

8. **Posita contra Hispania.**] Comp. preceding chapter, on the supposed extent of Spain in a northerly direction. The Silures inhabited Wales.

9. **Proximi Gallis, etc.**] 'Those who are nearest to the Gauls also resemble them.'

10. **Procurrentibus in diversa.**] Neighbouring countries jutting out in different directions (in diversa) would approximate very closely, would cccupy nearly the same *positio coeli*, and so would be subject to nearly the same climatic influences.

11. **In universum aestimanti.**] Comp. *Germ.* 6, in *universum aestimanti* plus apnd peditem robur.

12. **Superstitionum persuasiones.**] Sc. 'superstitious beliefs.' The meaning is that both the same rites (sacra) and the same beliefs prevailed in Britain as in Gaul. Comp. Caes. *B. G.* VI. 13. 'Superstitio' denoted to a Roman 'any *foreign* religious belief.' The reading of the MSS. 'persuasione' (retained by Oielli) hardly admits of explanation.

13. **In deposcendis...formido.**] Comp. Caesar *B. G.* III. 16, Ut ad bella suscipienda Gallorum alacer ac promptus est animus, sic mollis ac minime resistens ad calamitates perferendas mens eorum est.

14. **Praeferunt.**] 'Display.'

15. **Gallos quoque in bellis floruisse, etc.**] Comp. Caesar, *B. G.* passim, and Cic. *De Prov. Consul.* 13, Nemo de Republica nostra sapienter cogitavit jam inde ac principio hujus imperii, quin Galliam maxime timendam huic imperio putaret.

16. **Quales Galli fuerunt.**] Kritz takes *Galli* to be the complement not the subject of the sentence, and would translate 'such as *they* were when Gauls.' This seems unnecessary. The meaning is plain enough, if we suppose Tacitus to say—the Gauls before they were conquered were great warriors; but military spirit is incompatible with servitude. Servitude has destroyed it in the Gauls, has not yet done so with all the Britons; many of them still remain what the Gauls were.

CHAPTER XII

1. **Et curru proeliantur.**] Tacitus' meaning is that their troops generally consisted of infantry and cavalry, the former being the stronger force (in pedite robur); and that some tribes used chariots as well. Comp. Caesar, *B. G.* IV. 24, praemisso *equitatu et essedariis.* Comp. however, ch. 36, *covinnarius eques,* where the common reading is covinnarius *et* eques.

2. **Honestior auriga, etc.**] This is the reverse of the well-known Homeric usage, and that described by Caesar as practised by the Gauls (loc. cit.).

3. **Clientes propugnant.**] The meaning is not that the cliens (θεράπων) fights *in advance* of the chariot, but that he fights *from it;* sc. performs the part of the combatant, while the chief drives.

4. **Olim regibus parebant.]** In this Tacitus is in agreement with Caesar. See Caesar, *B. G.* v. 22.

5. **Per principes.]** 'Under the action of chiefs.'

6. **Factionibus et studiis.]** 'Factiones' signify the combinations on the part of the chiefs, 'studia' the partialities in the people to which they appealed. The words are to be taken as ablatives.

7. **Trahuntur.]** Either for 'distrahuntur,' the simple word for the compound according to a common Tacitean usage; or simply meaning 'are drawn,' as having no stability of purpose.

8. **Nec aliud...consulunt.]** Comp. Ch. 29, tandem docti commune periculum concordia propulsandum.

9. **Singuli pugnant...vincuntur.]** 'They fight singly, [and therefore] are all conquered.'

10. **Foedum.]** So *Hist.* I. 18, *foedum* imbribus diem.

11. **Asperitas frigorum abest.]** Comp. Caesar, *B. G.* v. 12, Loca sunt temperatiora quam in Gallia remissioribus frigoribus.

12. **Dierum spatia...mensuram.]** Pliny, *H. N.* II. 75, says that the longest day in Britain is seventeen hours in length.

13. **Scilicet extrema...nox cadit.]** The notion on which this explanation is founded was that night was the shadow cast by the earth. Comp. Plin. *H. N.* II. 7, Neque aliud esse noctem quam *terrae umbram.* This shadow as cast by the 'extrema et plana terrarum,' 'the flat extremities of the earth' (which, of course, is conceived of as a plane surface), would reach but to a small altitude (humilis); the darkness therefore would not extend very high, and while it more or less affected the earth would wholly fail to touch the higher regions (infra coelum et sidera nox cadit).

14. **Praeter oleam, &c.]** 'If we except the olive, &c.'

15. **Patiens frugum, fecundum.]** 'Admits of their growth and bears them in abundance.' Comp. *Germ.* 5, terra frugiferarum arborum *impatiens.*

16. **Proveniunt.]** 'Shoot forth,' 'grow.'

17. **Aurum et argentum.]** Caesar mentions only iron and lead among the metals of Britain. Strabo however (IV. 5. 2) enumerates *gold* and *silver* among them.

18. **Pretium victoriae.]** Comp. *Hist.* I. 11, Inermes provinciae......in pretium belli cessurae erant.

19. **Liventia.]** 'Of a blueish or leaden hue.' Pliny, *H. N.* IX. 35, says that the pearls of Britain are small and discoloured

(decolores).   Pearls are still found in considerable numbers in the aestuaries of some of the Scotch rivers.

20. **Expulsa.**] 'Thrown up from the sea.'

CHAPTER XIII.

1. **Ipsi Britanni.**] Sc. the inhabitants as opposed to the natural products of the island.

2. **Injuncta imperii munera.**] 'The services which the ruling power enjoins on its subjects.' To such would belong the furnishing of troops with provisions; all contributions not included in the regular tribute, forced labour, &c. Comp. Ch. 32, where some of these 'munera imperii' are specified.

3. **Si injuriae absint.**] Comp. Ch. 19, [Agricola] doctus parum profici armis si *injuriae* sequerentur.

4. **Jam domiti...serviant.**] Comp. what Galba is made to say in adopting Piso of the Romans themselves, *Hist.* 1. 16, imperaturus es hominibus qui nec totam servitutem pati possunt nec totam libertatem.

5. **Igitur.**] The last sentence, describing the degree to which Britain had been brought into subjection to the Roman power, suggests a *transition* to the writer's more immediate subject, a sketch of the military operations of Rome in the island previous to the arrival of Agricola.

6. **Britanniam ingressus, &c.**] Comp. Caesar. *B. G.* IV. 23—36, V. 8—23.

7. **Potest videri.**] 'Must be regarded.'

8. **Mox bella civilia.**] Sc. the civil wars which ended in the establishment of the first and second Triumvirates.

9. **Longa oblivio...in pace.**] Comp. *Ann.* IV. 5. where, in the list of legions, no mention is made of a force in Britain. During the civil war that followed on the death of Galba, no less than three legions were stationed in the island.

10. **Consilium.**] Comp. *Ann.* I. 11, addiderat [Augustus] consilium coercendi intra terminos imperii. The word may be rendered 'policy.'

11. **Praeceptum.**] Comp. *Ann.* I. 77, neque *fas* Tiberio infringere dicta ejus; *Ann.* IV. 37, where Tiberius is represented as saying of himself, qui omnia facta dictaque ejus *vice legis* observem.

12. **Ni velox...fuissent.**] The sentence is, of course highly elliptical. He conceived designs and (would have carried them out) had he not been, &c. We prefer to read 'mobilis poenitentiae' with Orelli to the reading 'mobili' which Kritz adopts. With the latter reading the meaning is (fuisset being

supplied out of fuissent in either case), 'had he not been swift to repent or change his purpose (velox poenitentiae) from the fickleness of his disposition (mobili ingenio).' Otherwise 'velox' is joined with 'ingenio,' and 'mobilis' with 'poenitentiae.' He was at once hasty in his impulses and easily moved to change. 'Mobilis' may agree either with Caesar, the nominative of the sentence, or with 'poenitentiae.' The phrase 'commotus ingenio' (*Ann.* VI. 45) is cited as parallel to 'ingenio mobili,' but it is at least as near akin to 'velox ingenio.'

13. **Ingentes ... fuissent.**] Comp. *Germ.* 37, *ingentes G. Caesaris minae* in ludibrium versae; *Hist.* IV. 15, Gaianarum expeditionum ludibrium.

14. **Auctor iterati operis.**] The MSS. read 'auctoritate operis.' As this gives no meaning, we have followed Kritz in adopting the conjecture of Wex. 'Iteratum opus' is the work of subduing Britain anew.

15. **Vespasiano.**] Comp. *Hist.* III. 44, Illic (in Britain) secundae legioni a Claudio praepositus et bello clarus egerat.

16. **Fortunae.**] This must be the greatness of Vespasian, not the success of Claudius, as Kritz appears to think.

17. **Monstratus fatis.**] We prefer with Orelli to take 'fatis' as a *dative* than with Kritz as an *ablative.* The half paradox of the future ruler being pointed out to the destinies which decreed his fortune is very characteristic of Tacitus. Vespasian's successful career in Britain commended him, so to speak, to destiny, as one worthy of higher distinction.

CHAPTER XIV.

1. **Proxima.**] Nearest (to the coast).

2. **Colonia.**] i. e. Camulodunum.

3. **Cogidumno.**] Nothing is known of this king.

4. **Ut.**] We have followed the reading of the MSS. putting ut before vetere, as we do not see any absolute necessity for altering it.

5. **Reges.**] Kings of this kind were the Tigranes mentioned, *Ann.* XIV. 26, Sohaemus, Antiochus and Agrippa, *Hist.* II. 81, Sido and Italicus, III. 21.

6. **Aucti officii.**] 'Of having enlarged the range of his duties' of his government. A governor's 'officium' was simply to administer his province as he received it; Gallus did something more by advancing military positions (castella) beyond the limit of former conquests.

7. Prosperas ... praesidiis.] 'Achieved the success of subduing tribes,' &c. Understand the ablatives 'subactis nationibus' &c. as the epexegesis of 'prosperas res.' Comp. for a precisely similar construction Ch. 22, Tertius expeditionum annus novas gentes aperuit *vastatis* usque ad Tanaum *nationibus.*

8. Firmatis praesidiis.] 'Firmare praesidia' is to place them in secure positions.

CHAPTER XV.

1. Britanni ... accendere.] A distinction is to be noted between 'agitare' and 'conferre.' The first denotes discussions in which *all* took part, the second, discussions and interviews of a more *private* nature. For the expression 'interpretando accendere,' comp. Livy, IV. 58, haec sua sponte *agitata* insuper tribuni plebis *accendunt.* 'Interpretando' means 'by discovering a common meaning or purpose in them.'

2. Ex facili.] A Graecism. Comp. ex insperato, ex aperto, ex affluenti &c. &c. Graecisms were characteristic of the silver age.

3. Singulos...reges.] Sc. the 'legatus,' before the organization of the province was completed, and before the procurators were introduced.

4. E quibus legatus ... saeviret.] The 'legatus' had the military 'imperium' which involved the 'jus gladii' and the power of inflicting capital punishment. The procurator could not take judicial cognisance of illegal acts and pass sentence on them, but it was his business to assess fines and see that they were paid into the 'fiscus.' The subjunctive (saeviret) is used to imply the *purpose* with which the legatus and procurator were set over the Britons; this, at least, was the *interpretatio* which the Britons themselves put on the matter. The rapacity of a procurator (Catus Decianus) is mentioned, *Ann.* XIV. 32, as the occasion of an outbreak in Britain.

5. Alterius manum ...miscere.] The first 'alterius' refers to the legatus, the second, to the procurator. The 'manus' of the legatus were officers and military attendants selected by him for the performance of special and confidential services. It nearly answers to our 'staff,' and it would chiefly consist of soldiers of a centurion's rank. It is alluded to Ch. 19, nec ex commendatione aut precibus *centurionem, milites ascire,* sed optimum quemque fidelissimum putare, in which passage the *milites* are what is here termed 'manus.' The 'servi' of the procurator, would be persons employed in collecting fines and debts, and were probably not soldiers. The passage may be thus rendered: 'The attendants and centurions of the one, the slaves of the other mingle violence and insult.' Comp. *Ann.* XIV. 31, where we are told that the kingdom of Prasatagus, king of the Iceni, was plundered by *centurions*, his house, by *slaves*. Orelli reads 'manus.' The centurions were, as it were, the 'hands' of the 'legatus.' So Cic. *In Verr.* II. 10, comites illi tui delecti *manus* erant tuae.

6. **In praelio &c. &c.**] The meaning is, in war it is the weak who suffer, whereas now matters are reversed, and we, the stronger, and braver, suffer at the hands of the coward, &c. &c.

7. **Ab ignavis ... imbellibus.**] Referring especially to the 'veterani' quartered in Camulodunum. Comp. the expression 'senum coloniae' in the speech of Calgacus, Ch. 32. These 'veterani' as we learn from *Ann.* XIV. 31, had thrust the people out of their houses and driven them from their estates.

8. **Quantulum.**] 'What a mere fraction.'

9. **Sic.**] Sc. by reckoning up and uniting their strength.

10. **Germanias.**] The plural is used for rhetorical effect, though the truth of the assertion was strictly limited to a portion of Lower Germany. The allusion is to the defeat and destruction of the army of Varus.

11. **Illis.**] Sc. the Romans.

12. **Plus impetus.**] 'More fury' (*C* and *B*).

13. **In ejusmodi consiliis.**] 'In such deliberations,' or we may perhaps translate 'in such designs,' i. e. where such designs are in question.

CHAPTER XVI.

The events related in this Chapter occurred A. D. 61. They are related at greater length, *Ann.* XIV. 31—38.

1. **Instincti.**] The word has a *middle* sense. 'Rousing themselves, &c.'

2. **Consectati.**] The notion of the word is that of a searching and vindictive pursuit.

3. **Coloniam.**] Camulodunum.

4. **In barbaris.**] Sc. usual among barbarians.

5. **Ira et victoria.**] 'The rage of victory.'

6. **Veteri patientiae restituit.**] 'Brought back to its old obedience.' 'Restituit,' in our reading of the passage must be taken for 'restituisset.'

7. **Tenentibus arma plerisque, &c.]** '*Though* many held arms,' &c. This clause is parenthetical.

8. **Propius…timor.]** 'Propius' (the reading of the MSS. for which Wex and Kritz read *proprius*) seems defensible, though no doubt 'propior' is what we should have expected. It must be construed with 'agitabat.' 'Fear from the legatus (sc. fear of which he was the source) was more urgently harassing them,' &c. &c. Punishment to those who were conscious of the guilt of rebellion seemed more imminent than to others.

9. **Ni quamquam, &c.]** This is the reading of Orelli and Wex. The passage is difficult and confused. The objection to the reading *ne* quamquam, &c. is that it obliges us either to take the words *egregius cetera* as expressing the *Britons'* opinion about Paulinus, which Tacitus would hardly have cared to mention, or else, as very obscurely and clumsily interposed. We have, in fact, but a choice of difficulties, and the reading adopted appears to present the least. Reading 'ni' we should give the meaning thus; 'He would have brought the province back, &c. had he not been disposed thus to act.'

10. **Ut suae cujusque injuriae ultor.]** 'As one who avenged every wrong as if it was his own.'

11. **Durius.]** 'Too harshly.'

12. **Petronius Turpilianus.]** He was legatus from A.D. 62—64. See *Ann.* XIV. 39, *Hist.* I. 6, where his murder at the beginning of Galba's reign is recorded.

13. **Compositis prioribus.]** Comp. *Ann.* I. 45, *compositis* praesentibus. *Priora* refers to the late outbreak of the Britons and its suppression by Paulinus. There would still be much lingering irritation and discontent in Britain; this, Petronius allayed, and thus effectually restored peace and tranquillity.

14. **Trebellio Maximo.]** Comp. *Hist.* I. 60. Trebellius was governor of Britain from A.D. 64 to 69.

15. **Nullis castrorum experimentis.]** 'A man with no actual experience of campaigns.'

16. **Curandi.]** 'Curare' is used both of military commands and of civil administration. Comp. *Ann.* XI. 22, duo additi (quaestores) qui Romae *curarent.*

17. **Ignoscere vitiis blandientibus.]** 'To shew indulgence to vices as they became attractive.' It is best, we think, to take 'vitiis' as a dative. Comp. Ch. 21, paullatim discessum ad *delenimenta vitiorum.*

18. **Civilium armorum.]** The civil wars which followed the death of Nero, A. D. 69, (1) between Galba and Otho, (2) between Otho and Vitellius, (3) between Vitellius and Vespasian.

19. **Discordia laboratum.]** 'Troubles arose from mutiny.' See Ch. 7, and *Hist.* I. 60, which passages shew that the allusion is to the quarrels between Trebellius, and Coelius who commanded the 20th legion. Tacitus, however, says *Hist.* I. 9, non sane aliae legiones per omnes civilium bellorum motus innocentius egerunt.

20. **Quum assuetus ... lasciviret.]** 'When a soldiery accustomed to campaigns were demoralised by indolence.'

21. **Praecario praefuit.]** 'Governed on sufferance.'

22. **Vettius Bolanus.]** See *Hist.* II. 65, 97. Bolanus was sent A. D. 70 to Britain by Vitellius, and under him Agricola commanded the 20th legion. Comp. Ch. 8.

23. **Agitavit Britanniam disciplina.]** Sc. he undertook no campaigns, which would have required the enforcement of strict discipline among the troops.

24. **Petulantia.]** 'Insubordination,' such as would lead to wanton outrages.

25. **Innocens.]** The word especially denotes, 'free from the guilt of rapacity.' In this respect Bolanus was a contrast to Trebellius who is said (*Hist.* I. 60) to have been per avaritiam ac sorde contemptus exercitui invisusque.

CHAPTER XVII.

1. **Recuperavit.]** 'Restored to unity.' There is a reference in the word to the civil wars which had distracted the world, and also, it would seem, to Vespasian's superiority over his predecessors, which almost gave him a right to empire. He seemed, as it were, to recover what was his own.

2. **Aut victoria ... bello.]** Sc. either conquered or ravaged. If he was not successful everywhere he fought everywhere; nothing escaped his reach (amplexus).

3. **Et Cerialis ... licebat.]** Orelli's correction *sed* sustinuit, &c. (which we have adopted) is the simplest, though there is a strong probability that there is a considerable lacuna after obruisset. We incline to think that by *alterius* successoris Frontinus is meant, and not Agricola, as Wex insists, on the ground that 'alter' cannot be used for 'alius.' He says that 'alter successor' can mean only secundus a Ceriali, that is, Agricola. It seems too much to assert that in no case can alter approach

in meaning to alius, and it certainly is unlikely that Tacitus would even suggest a comparison between Cerialis and Agricola, as by this interpretation he is made to do. For the expression 'curam famamque obruisset' comp. Ch. 46, multos veterum oblivio *obruit.* 'Obruisset' (would have completely extinguished) is a stronger word than obscurasset, by which it has been explained. By 'molem' we are to understand the difficulty of the work imposed on Frontinus, who had to complete what Cerialis had so ably begun. Comp. its use *Ann.* I. 45, haud minor *moles* supererat ob ferociam quintae et vicesimae legionis; *Hist.* III. 46, ne externa *moles* utrimque ingrueret. There remains some difficulty about the words 'quantum licebat.' Their collocation seems to require that they should be construed with 'vir magnus,' though Wex and Kritz take them with 'sustinuit molem,' understanding them to mean that Frontinus, so far as the difficulties of his position permitted, carried out the arduous task which devolved on him. It is possible however that Tacitus, although in this very chapter he has admitted that under Vespasian there were 'magni duces,' may be hinting at that Emperor's well-known parsimony which would have the effect of discouraging costly and difficult enterprises, or that he may wish to imply generally that an imperial *régime* is sure to set limits on greatness. Julius Frontinus had been praetor urbanus. He was probably at this time a praetorian legatus in Britain, and seems to have commanded a legion in a different part of the country from that where the operations of Cerialis had been conducted. He was the author of two works which have come down to us, one on military stratagems, the other, on aqueducts. Pliny (*Ep.* IV. 8, 3), speaks of him in high terms.

4. **Eluctatus.**] Comp. *Hist.* III. 59, vix quieto agmine nives *eluctantibus,* &c. &c.

CHAPTER XVIII.

1. **Media aestate.**] A.D. 78, the tenth year of Vespasian's reign.

2. **Velut omissa expeditione.**] Sc. 'under the impression that campaigns were over.'

3. **Ad securitatem ...... verterentur.**] The MSS. fluctuate between *verterentur* and *uterentur,* which latter Orelli reads, construing it with the ablative 'omissa expeditione.' But 'verti ad aliquid' is a well known phrase, and suits the present passage. Comp. *Hist.* V. 11, Romani ad oppugnandum *reversi, Ann.* XIV. 38, omni aetate ad bellum *versa.* So here *verterentur* has a middle sense. There is no zeugma, since *verti* ad securitatem, *verti* ad occasionem, are both legitimate expressions. 'Securitatem,' 'carelessness :' 'occasionem,' 'an opportunity for attack.'

4. **Alam in finibus suis agentem.**] 'A detachment of auxiliary cavalry quartered in their territory.' Agere often has this meaning in Tacitus. Comp. *Hist.* I. 74, eas, quae Lugduni *agebant*, copias.

5. **Obtriverat.**] The word implies *sudden* and *complete* destruction.

6. **Erecta provincia.**] 'The province was stirred into a commotion.'

7. **Quibus bellum volentibus erat.**] 'Those who wished for war.' A well-known Graecism.

8. **Quanquam, &c.**] The clause introduced by quanquam ends at videbatur.

9. **Numeri.**] Sc. troops not regularly enrolled in the legion or forming part of it. The word, in the time of the Emperors, had come in fact to designate the various forces of infantry and cavalry which could not be strictly included among the legionaries, though they were attached to them. See *Hist.* I. 6, multi ad hoc *numeri*, I. 87, in *numeros* legionis. The term occurs from time to time in Pliny and Suetonius.

10. **Praesumpta ...... quies.**] 'Though repose for that year had been counted on by the soldiers.' 'Praesumere' 'to enjoy by anticipation.' Comp. *Ann.* XI. 7, quem illum tanta superbia esse ut aeternitatem famae spe *praesumat?* Pliny (*Epp.* IV. 15) uses in this sense the derived noun 'praesumptio.' Rerum quas assequi cupias *praesumptio* ipsa jucunda est.

11. **Tarda et contraria.**] These words are in apposition with transvecta aestas, sparsi......numeri, praesumpta......quies, three sources of delay just mentioned. 'Tarda,' 'causing delay.'

12. **Custodiri suspecta.**] 'That suspected points should be watched,' sc. tribes imperfectly conquered, or likely to revolt.

13. **Vexillis.**] By 'vexilla' are meant what above are termed 'numeri.' They must not be confounded with the 'vexillarii' or veterans. Tacitus uses the word elsewhere with this meaning. Comp. *Ann.* II. 78, Piso ...... *vexillum* tironum in Syriam euntium intercipit, *Hist.* I. 70, Germanorum *vexillis*, II. 11, equitum *vexilla*. In this case, they would appear, from the mention of *auxilia* immediately afterwards, to have been *Roman* troops, though the term, as it is clear from *Hist.* I. 70, was not restricted to such troops.

14. **Erexit aciem.**] 'Led his troops up the hill.' Comp. Ch. 36, *erigere* in colles aciem.

15. **Instandum famae.**] 'That he must follow up the prestige of success.' Comp. *Hist.* III. 52, *instandum* coeptis ; V. 15, *instare* fortunae.

16. **Prout prima cessissent.**] 'In proportion as his first attempts had succeeded.' Comp. *Hist.* II. 20, gnarus, ut initia belli proveniissent, famam in cetera fore. 'Prima' here = initia belli.

17. **Ut in dubiis consiliis.**] 'As happens in imperfectly matured plans.'

18. **Ratio et constantia, &c.**] 'The forethought and decision,' &c.

19. **Quibus nota vada.**] Agricola's auxiliaries (among whom, as appears from Ch. 36, were Batavians) could hardly have known these particular seas, so that by 'vada' it seems best to understand 'shallows, fords' generally. The Batavians were famous swimmers, as we learn *Hist.* IV. 12, *Ann.* II. 8. We must suppose that the channel separating Anglesea from the main land must have undergone a great change since that period. If we comp. *Ann.* XIV. 29, we see that the water was shallow. Flat-bottomed boats were provided. The cavalry forded part of the way and had occasion to swim only in the deeper places (altiores inter undas).

20. **Quod tempus...transigunt.**] 'A time which others pass in idle show and a round of ceremonies.' 'Officia' denote the various compliments and honours paid by the provincials to a new governor on his arrival among them. In the word 'ambitus' there is the notion of courting these distinctions.

21. **Expeditionem...continuisse.**] (He did not) 'give the name of campaign or conquest to the having kept the conquered in subjection.'

22. **Laureatis.**] Sc. litteris. The noun is rarely omitted.

23. **Aestimantibus...tacuisset.**] 'In the eyes of those who reckoned what expectations he must have for the future, to have been silent about such great deeds.' It seems best (with Kritz) to take aestimantibus as a dative.

CHAPTER XIX.

1. **Animorum provinciae prudens.**] 'Well acquainted with the temper of the province.' 'Prudens' here = gnarus. Comp, *Hist.* II. 25, Celsus doli *prudens* repressit suos. Possibly in animorum there is the notion of high spirit, a meaning often found in the plural of animus.

2. **Injuriae.**] This is the correction of Puteolanus for 'inouriae,' which the MSS. have, and it is the reading of most recent editors. Incuriae seems hardly defensible. The plural of

incuria is nowhere found, nor does the idea of 'official *negli-gence*' suit the context so well as that of oppression and in-justice.

3. **Domum suam.**] Sc. his servants and subordinates generally.

4. **Nihil...publicae rei.**] 'He transacted no public busi-ness through freedmen and slaves.' Understand 'agere.'

5. **Non studiis...ascire.**] 'He did not select his centu-rions or attendant soldiers according to his own personal inclina-tions or the recommendations or requests (of others).' 'Ascire' (due to Puteolanus for the reading of the MSS. nescire, which Orelli retains and endeavours to explain) seems to be unquestion-ably the right reading and is now generally adopted. By 'cen-turionem, milites' we are to understand the same as by 'centu-riones, mauum (legati),' Ch. 15, where see note. 'Ascire,' ex-pressing as it does deliberate choice and selection, is the word required in such a connexion. Under the head of 'attendant soldiers' would be included lictors, apparitors, clerks, secretaries, purveyors of corn, &c. &c. These persons were comprehended under the common designation ' *cohors accensorum*,' and being released from all strictly military duties were termed 'benefici-arii.'

6. **Non omnia exsequi.**] 'He did not punish in every case.'

7. **Severitatem commodare.**] This is something like a zeugma, though we find a similar use of '*commodare*,' Ovid, *Amores*, I. 8, 86, *Commodat* illusis numina surda Venus.

8. **Nec poena...esse.**] Construe 'poena' as an ablative depending on 'contentus.' This, though a sort of zeugma, seems better than joining it, as Kritz does, with 'commodare.'

9. **Aequalitate...munerum.**] *Munera* denote the various burdens imposed by the Romans on the Britons. These fell under two heads, (1) contributions of corn, (2) the payment of a money-tribute. The first would necessarily be vexatious in districts where corn was scarce. For this difficulty Agricola found a remedy by requiring in such cases as an equivalent pay-ment the average price which corn fetched in parts where it was more plentiful. This was done by means of an assessment, 'aestimatio frumenti,' as it was termed, a phrase we meet with Cic. *Verr.* III. 82, where the whole matter is explained.

10. **In quaestum.**] 'With a view to gain.'

11. **Namque per ludibrium...cogebantur.**] We adhere to the reading of the MSS. aud of Orelli, which Kritz also retains. We understand the passage as describing one of the

cunning methods of extortion to which Roman governors had been in the habit of resorting in districts scantily furnished with corn. Instead of accepting a money-equivalent for the 'frumentum imperatum,' they compelled the Britons to purchase corn from the Roman granaries up to the required amount. Of course they could fix their price, and had the purchasers at their mercy. The corn would thus be often bought at an excessive price, and when bought it still remained in the Roman granaries, so that the whole affair was a 'ludibrium.' Hence the Britons are said (1) 'emere ultro frumenta,' that is, to buy corn needlessly and under very provoking circumstances, and (2) 'ludere pretio,' a phrase which has been variously interpreted, but which seems to mean, 'to be going through a farce with the price,' inasmuch as they were paying dear for what after all the seller kept in his possession. Wex's conjecture 'luere' for 'ludere' which he explains by 'luere imperata' ignores the ordinary usage of 'luere' which requires to be followed by an accusative of the object. In Livy, xxx. 37, the reading ('pecunia luere') which he quotes is doubtful. Kritz reads 'recludere,' and explains the passage as meaning that the Britons had to buy their corn out of the granaries and then shut it up (i. e. see it shut up) again in them. But this use of 'recludere' is very questionable.

12. **Devortia itinerum...deferrent.**] 'Places lying out of the regular roads and distant parts of the country were appointed, in order that states, with winter camps close to them, might have to convey corn into remote and out of the way districts.' Here we have another method of Roman extortion, applicable to the *corn-growing* districts. The inhabitants, finding it troublesome and costly to carry their corn to a distance, would be glad to commute the required contribution for a money payment fixed by the governor. This device is specially mentioned in the Verrine Speeches, III. 82, Instituerunt semper ad ultima ac difficillima loca apportandum frumentum imperare ubi vecturae difficultate ad quam vellent aestimationem pervenirent.

13. **Quod omnibus in promptu erat.**] Sc. 'what under fair conditions would have been easy for all.' Understand by 'quod' the furnishing of the 'frumentum imperatum,' which under an equitable system would have been by no means burdensome where corn was plentiful.

CHAPTER XX.

1. **Haec.**] Sc. these abuses.

2. **Egregiam......circumdedit.**] 'Invested peace with great glory.' Comp. *Hist.* IV. 11, qui principatus *inanem ei famam circumdarent;* Dial. 37, hanc illi *famam circumdederunt.*

3. **Intolerantia.**] Cicero, *Cluent.* XL. 112, couples this word with 'superbia.' It may be rendered 'harshness.'

4. **Multus in agmine.**] Sc. he continually marched on foot with his troops. 'Agmen,' 'a column in marching order.' Comp. Sallust's description of Sulla, *Jug.* 96, in *agmine* atque ad vigilias *multus* adesse.

5. **Modestiam.**] 'Obedience,' 'subordination.' The word is often applied to obedience to military discipline.

6. **Disjectos.**] 'Stragglers.' Opposed to 'modesti' (the well-disciplined).

7. **Nihil interim...quominus.**] Comp. for the construction Ch. 27, nihil ex arrogantia remittere *quominus* juventutem armarent.

8. **Irritamenta.**] A stronger and more expressive word than 'incitamenta' or 'illecebrae.' Comp. the Greek ἐρεθίσματα. *Irritationes* is similarly used *Germ.* 19, nullis conviviorum *irritationibus* corruptae.

9. **Ex aequo egerant.**] 'Had been independent.' Comp. *Hist.* IV. 64, aut *ex aequo agetis* aut aliis imperabitis.

10. **Ut.**] *Here* equivalent to quanta.

11. **Nova pars.**] 'Nova,' sc. recently conquered. Understand after 'nova pars,' praesidiis castellisque circumdata fuit.

CHAPTER XXI.

1. **Sequens hiems.**] A.D. 79—80, the first of which was the year of Vespasian's death.

2. **Bello faciles.**] The choice seems to lie between the reading 'bello,' which we follow with Kritz (the MSS. have 'in bello'), and 'in bella' which Orelli adopts. '*Facilis*' is joined with the dative, *Ann.* II. 27, juvenem improvidum et *facilem* inanibus, and *Hist.* II. 17, longa pax fregerat *faciles occupantibus.* In both of these passages, however, it seems to have the passive sense of 'easily acted on' rather than the active meaning of 'promptly and readily turning to a thing.'

3. **Publice.**] Sc. by grants from the public treasury.

4. **Ingenia...anteferre.**] 'He showed a preference for the natural powers of the Britons over the industry of the Gauls.' (*C.* and *B.*) Orelli gives a different, and, we think, very doubtful meaning to 'anteferre,' and understands the passage thus,

'he trained the natural powers of the Britons up to a higher point than had been reached by the industry of the Gauls.' He thus makes 'anteferre' equivalent to 'promovere,' a use of the word to which we can find no parallel.

5. **Delenimenta vitiorum.**] 'Attractive accompaniments of vice.'

6. **Apud imperitos.**] 'Imperiti' are here persons who looked at the matter merely from the surface.

7. **Humanitas.**] 'Civilisation.'

8. **Pars servitutis.**] Comp. for a like sentiment *Hist.* IV. 64, Instituta cultumque patrium resumite, abruptis voluptatibus, quibus Romani plus adversus subjectos quam armis valent.

CHAPTER XXII.

1. **Tertius...annus.**] A.D. 80.

2. **Tanaum.**] This is the reading of the MSS., for which Orelli and Ritter read *Taus*, after Puteolanus from a marginal gloss in one of the MSS., and understand by it the frith of Tay. We think it unlikely that Agricola had as yet advanced so far north. His campaign of this year, we have little doubt, was confined to the country *south* of Bodotria, the frith of Forth, which he does not appear to have crossed till his 6th year (see Ch. 25). Nor again can we think that by the Taus is meant the Tweed, to which the word 'aestuarium' could be hardly applied. Agricola too by this time had probably pushed into Caledonia. Perhaps, as suggested by Wex, we are to understand the mouth of the North Tyne at Dunbar. The fact that '*Tan*' is a Keltic name for running water confirms the reading 'Tanaus.'

3. **Conflictatum saevis tempestatibus.**] Comp. *Hist.* III. 59, sed foeda hieme per transitum Apennini *conflictatus* exercitus. 'Shattered' is perhaps the best English equivalent to 'conflictatus.'

4. **Periti.**] 'Men of experience.'

5. **Pactione.**] Sc. 'capitulation.'

6. **Annuis copiis.**] 'With provisions for the year.' Comp. Ch. 25, mixti *copiis* et laetitia.

7. **Sibi quisque praesidio.**] Understand by 'quisque' every commander of a 'castellum.'

8. **Hibernis eventibus.**] 'By successes in winter.' Comp. Ch. 8, majoribus copiis ex *eventu* praefecit, 'eventus' being used for a prosperous result.

9. **Nec...avidus intercepit.**] 'He never in a covetous spirit appropriated to himself,' &c. &c.

10. **Seu centurio seu praefectus.**] The *centurion* was a legionary officer, the '*praefectus*' one connected with the auxiliaries (*cohortes alaeque*).

11. **Incorruptum.**] 'Impartial.'

12. **Injucundus.**] Horace (*Sat.* I. 3, 85) uses insuavis in the same sense. 'Injucundus' is not quite so strong a word as *durus* would have been.

13. **Nihil supererat secretum ut, &c.**] This, the reading of the MSS. (for which secretum et silentium were commonly substituted) is retained by Kritz, and may, we think, well mean that there was no reserve, nothing hidden, or as it were lurking behind, in the displeasure of Agricola. His anger was at once and fully expressed; none was kept back to burst out on some future occasion. 'Secretum' has here much the same meaning as 'reconditum,' a word which Tacitus uses in a very similar connexion, *Ann.* I. 69, accendebat haec...Sejanus, peritia morum Tiberii, odia in longum jaciens, quae *reconderet*, auctaque promeret. It may be that a contrast is suggested between Agricola and Domitian who is described, Ch. 42, as quo obscurior, eo implacabilior.

14. **Offendere quam odisse.**] Sc. to give open offence rather than to cherish hatred.

CHAPTER XXIII.

1. **Quarta aestas.**] A.D. 81.

2. **Obtinendis quae percucurrerat.**] 'In securing the places through which he had rapidly moved.'

3. **Clota et Bodotria.**] Sc. the friths of Clyde and Forth.

4. **Diversi maris.**] 'Of an opposite sea.' 'Diversus' here = contrarius.'

5. **Revectae.**] Sc. carried back from the sea into the land. The notion is that the two estuaries are carried by the strength of the tides out of their natural channel and forced to a great distance (per immensum) inland.

6. **Omnis propior sinus.**] Sc. the country to the south of Clota and Bodotria, nearer (propior) to the Roman province. 'sinus' may denote a tract of country with a winding and indented shore. Comp. *Germ.* I, latos *sinus*, and see note 5.

7. **Velut in aliam insulam.]** Sc. Caledonia to the north of Clota and Bodotria, which all but divided it from its southern portion.

CHAPTER XXIV.

1. **Quinto expeditionum anno.]** A.D. 82.

2. **Nave prima.]** This is susceptible of the following meanings; (1) the *first* Roman vessel which had visited those parts; (2) the first vessel which ventured to sea in the early spring; (3) the *foremost* vessel of the fleet; (4) the *first* vessel which Agricola had as yet had occasion to employ. The choice seems to us to lie between (1) and (3), and on the whole we prefer (1), both grammatically as the simplest, and as best suiting the context. It is far from probable that Agricola quitted Britain for the winter and returned in the spring, as has been supposed. By 'transgressus' we understand that he crossed Clota. Wex, seeing the obscurity of the passage, would read, navi in proxima, and observes that *navi*, as distinguished from 'nave,' means simply 'by sea,' and is in fact used adverbially, as *vesperi, luci, &c.*

3. **In spem.]** Sc. with the prospect of some advantage. The preposition 'in' is similarly used, Ch. 8, nec Agricola unquam *in* suam famam gestis exsultavit.

4. **Medio inter Britanniam atque Hispaniam.]** Comp. Ch. 10, Britannia in occidentem *Hispaniae* obtenditur.

5. **Gallico mari opportuna.]** 'Easily accessible from the seas of Gaul.'

6. **Valentissimam imperii partem.]** Sc. Britain, Gaul, Spain and Upper and Lower Germany. The special reference in 'valentissimam' is to the *military* resources of these countries. We find, *Hist.* III. 53, Gaul and Spain described as the most powerful (*valentissimam*) part of the world, and the Britons, Ch. 12, are spoken of as *validissimae* gentes.

7. **Magnis invicem usibus miscuerit.]** 'Has united with great mutual advantages.' The subjunctive seems meant to express the writer's own notion of Agricola's views.

8. **Cultusque.]** Sc. 'the general mode of life.'

9. **Haud multum...cogniti.]** We prefer this reading to 'differt in melius,' which, though adopted by some recent editors, after Muretus, makes Tacitus responsible for a strange and unaccountable statement. We understand him to mean that so far as he could speak on the matter, the climate and population of

Hibernia resembled those of Britain, but that its coasts and harbours were better known than the island itself. This we take to be the meaning of *melius.* It would be absurd to suppose that it meant that the coasts of Hibernia were better known than those of Britain. Perhaps 'melius cogniti' may be rightly rendered, 'are tolerably well known.'

10. **Agricola...exceperat.**] The emperor Claudius, according to Dio, LX. 19, availed himself of a similar incident for the invasion of Britain, which he undertook at the solicitation of a refugee chief, Bericus.

11. **Ex eo.**] Sc. Agricola. Orelli strangely understands the 'regulus' mentioned above.

CHAPTER XXV.

1. **Ceterum.**] The word has a disjunctive force. This year Agricola's operations were transferred to the east coast.

2. **Sextum officii annum.**] A. D. 83, the third year of Domitian's reign.

3. **Amplexus.**] The word is to be understood in the same sense as in Ch. 17, Magnamque Brigantum partem aut victoria *amplexus* est aut bello, and denotes actual campaigns, not merely plans and designs.

4. **Infesta hostilis exercitus itinera.**] This is the reading of the best MSS. and is followed by Orelli and Kritz. By 'hostilis exercitus' we understand the Roman army, whose marches (itinera) through an enemy's country would be beset with danger (infesta). 'Infestus' often has a passive as well as an active sense.

5. **In partem virium.**] 'To form part of his force.'

6. **Egregia specie.**] 'With a remarkably imposing appearance.' Comp. a similar passage *Ann.* II. 6, naves augebantur alacritate militum in *speciem* ac terrorem.

7. **Impelleretur.**] 'Was being hurried on.'

8. **Misti copiis et laetitia.**] 'Copiae' here, as Ch. 22 (annuis copiis) and elsewhere, means 'provisions.' It is best to take 'copiis et laetitia' as a hendiadis. The meaning is that the soldiers and sailors mingled in merry gatherings over their meals.

9. **Ad manus.**] 'To force,' 'resistance.'

10. **Oppugnare.**] Construe this with 'adorti,' 'having attempted to storm,' &c.

5--2

11.   **Ut provocantes.**]   'As being the challengers.'

12.   **Pluribus agminibus.**]   'By several lines of march.'

13.   **Superante numero et peritia, &c.**]   'By superior numbers and superior knowledge of the localities,' &c.

CHAPTER XXVI.

1.   **Nonam legionem ut maxime invalidam.**] The ninth legion had been all but destroyed in the rising of the Britons under Boadicea (*Ann.* XIV. 32).   Its ranks, however, as we learn from *Ann.* XIV. 38, were shortly afterwards recruited with soldiers from Germany; but this may have been done very incompletely. At any rate, the Britons might well suppose the legion to have been comparatively weak.

2.   **Vestigiis insecutus.**]   Comp. Livy, VI. 32, quum Romanus exercitus prope *vestigiis sequeretur*, and IX. 45, pergunt hostem *vestigiis sequi.*

3.   **Assultare.**] The word specially denotes the rapid movements of cavalry or light-armed troops.   Comp. *Ann.* XII. 35, telis *assultantes*; XIII. 40, *assultare* ex diverso Tiridates, non usque ad ictum teli, &c.

4.   **Propinqua luce.**]   'The dawn approaching.'

5.   **Signa.**]   Sc. the eagles of the legions, which were preceded by the cavalry and light troops.

6.   **Securi pro salute.**]   'Having no fears for their safety.' Comp. *Hist.* IV. 58, Numquam apud vos verba feci aut pro vobis sollicitior aut *pro me securior.*

7.   **Ultro erupere.**]   'They (the soldiers of the 9th legion) actually sallied forth to the attack.'   'Ultro' gives the notion which we express by saying 'the tables were suddenly turned.'

8.   **Utroque exercitu.**]   Sc. the besieged army (the 9th legion) and the army which Agricola brought up to the rescue.

CHAPTER XXVII.

1.   **Cujus...ferox.**]   'Emboldened by their knowledge of this, and by the fame it excited.'   'Cujus' refers to 'victoria,' or rather, perhaps, to the decisive character of their success, of which we are told in the preceding sentence.

2.   **Illi modo...sapientes.**]   Sc. those who, ch. 25, were described as 'ignavi specie prudentium.'

3. **Iniquissima...imputantur.**] We meet with a similar sentiment, Sallust. *Jug.* 53, in victoria vel ignavis gloriari licet ; adversae res etiam bonos detractant.

4. **Occasione et arte, &c.**] 'By the general's skilful use of an opportunity.' The word 'elusos' (baffled) is received into the text by Kritz, as on the whole the most plausible conjecture. It suits the passage, and it seems to be at any rate better than the 'superati' of Ritter. This, however, is a passage in which the text cannot be restored with anything like certainty. It has been attempted to emend it as follows, non virtutem, sed occasionem et artem ducis rati, which is ingenious, but hardly satisfactory.

5. **Conspirationem.**] 'A confederacy.'

CHAPTER XXVIII.

1. **Usipiorum.**] See *Germ.* c. 32. In *Ann.* I. 51 they are called Usipetes, and are mentioned with the Bructeri and Tubantes as attacking the army of Germanicus on its retreat.

2. **Per Germanias.**] Sc. the provinces of Upper and Lower Germany.

3. **Occiso centurione, &c.**] The adventures of this Usipian cohort with these particulars are related by Dio, LXVI. 20. It would appear that the cohort was a part of the force which, as we are told Ch. 24, Agricola posted in that part of Britain which looks towards Ireland.

4. **Ad tradendam disciplinam.**] 'To impart discipline.' Vegetius, in his work on the Roman army (I. 13), speaks of 'annorum doctores' and 'campi doctores,' whose business it was to instruct newly-levied troops in their various military duties.

5. **Habebantur.**] Sc. were kept in the camp. Comp. for this use of 'haberi' *Ann.* XIII. 30, praefectus remigum qui Ravennae *haberentur.*

6. **Remigante.**] Sc. 'directing the rowers.'

7. **Praevehebantur.**] For 'praetervehebantur' as *Ann.* II. 6, Rhenus...Germaniam *praevehitur.*

8. **Mox ad aquam, &c.**] Many attempts have been made on this corrupt passage, without, as far as we can see, a satisfactory result. The common reading, mox hac atque illa rapti et cum plerisque, is founded on the very doubtful conjecture of Rhenanus. The word aquam, however, appears in all the MSS. and is accordingly retained by all recent editors. Kritz (whose

reading we have followed, as perhaps closer to the MSS. than any other) has adopted with slight modifications a suggestion of Haase, and interprets 'ad aquam' to mean 'in aquatione' and utilia as equivalent to utensilia (provisions), a use of the word which he thinks is confirmed by two passages of Sallust, *Hist. Frag.* II. 50, utilia parare, and *Jug.* 86, armis aliisque utilibus naves onerat. His explanation, however, of ad aquam seems very far-fetched, and, on the whole, we fear the passage remains hopelessly corrupt. Ritter reads 'ob aquam atque utensilia separati.' Roth's reading is perhaps as good as any, ad aquam et quae usui rapienda cum plerisque, &c.

9. **Eo ad extremum inopiae.]** Construe 'inopiae' with eo. 'Ad extremum,' 'at last.'

10. **Infirmissimos...vescerentur.]** They first fed on the weakest; then were reduced to draw lots for the healthy.

11. **Primum a Suevis...sunt.]** Some were taken by the Suevi, some by the Frisii. Tacitus does not mean that there were two successive captures of the same persons.

12. **In nostram ripam.]** Sc. the western bank of the Rhine.

13. **Mutatione ementium.]** Sc. by being resold by those who bought them.

14. **Indicium tanti casus.]** 'The disclosure of such an adventure.'

CHAPTER XXIX.

1. **Initio aestatis.]** Sc. A.D. 84.

2. **Ambitiose.]** Sc. with the affectation of stoical indifference. 'Ambitiosus' denotes that a thing is done for effect. Comp. Ch. 42, *ambitiosa* morte inclaruerunt.

3. **Rursus.]** 'On the other hand.'

4. **Bellum inter remedia erat.]** 'War was one of his sources of relief.' Comp. what is said, *Ann.* IV. 8, of Tiberius after the death of his son Drusus, se fortiora solatia e complexu reipublicae petivisse.

5. **Incertum terrorem.]** 'A vague panic.' The Britons would be uncertain as to the point whence the attack would come.

6. **Expedito exercitu.]** 'With an army unencumbered by baggage.'

7. **Longa pace exploratos.**] Sc. 'tried by a long period of peace.'

8. **Grampium.**] We have retained with Orelli and Ritter the more familiar form (which has some MS. authority), instead of Graupium, which Wex and Kritz read after one of the Vatican MSS. It seems to be a case in which there is some reason for declining to adhere strictly to MSS.

9. **Legationibus et foederibus.**] These words may of course be taken as a hendiadis. They may however be meant to convey two distinct ideas—the sending envoys to conclude treaties and get help, and the reminding states with whom treaties already existed of their obligations.

10. **Cruda ac viridis senectus.**] Comp. Virg. *Aen.* VI. 304, *cruda* deo *viridisque senectus*. 'Crudus,' 'fresh,' 'full of blood.'

11. **Sua quisque decora gestantes.**] The word 'decora' seems to include spoils taken from an enemy and rewards conferred by the chieftains on their followers.

12. **Locutus fertur.**] By the word 'fertur' Tacitus implies that he is himself the author of the following speech.

CHAPTER XXX.

1. **Necessitatem nostram.**] 'Our desperate position.'

2. **Magnus mihi animus est.**] 'I have great confidence. 'Animus' is here almost equivalent to 'spes' or 'fiducia.' There seems to be a studied simplicity about the expression.

3. **Nullae ultra terrae.**] 'There are no lands beyond us.' Comp. Ch. 10, septentrionalia ejus, *nullis contra terris*, vasto atque aperto mari pulsantur.

4. **Priores pugnae.**] Sc. previous battles of other tribes with the Romans.

5. **Spem ac subsidium, &c.**] A hendiadis for spem subsidii. The meaning is, that the Britons, though unsuccessful in former battles, still had hopes of being able to fall back upon us in their last extremity. 'Former engagements, &c. continued to leave a hope of succour from our resources,' &c.

6. **Nobilissimi.**] Sc. as being a pure and unmixed people. Comp. Caesar, *B. G.* v. 15, who says that the interior of Britain was occupied by a population which described itself as autochthonous (*natos in insula*).

7. **Iique.**] This seems a better reading than eoque, as it is not easy to see how the nobility and greatness of a people should be the cause of their occupying the remotest regions (penetralia) of a country. It has been strangely enough suggested that there is an implied comparison between such a people and jewels and treasures which are stowed away in secret places. If 'eoque' be read, it must mean that an indigenous population was likely to linger longest in the least accessible parts of a country.

8. **Servientium litora.**] Sc. the shores of Gaul.

9. **Oculos quoque … habebamus.**] 'We kept our very eyes unpolluted by the contagious touch of tyranny.'

10. **Sinus famae.**] We are inclined to think that this expression means the protection which the fame of their untried valour had hitherto lent them. The remoteness of their situation, and all the exaggeration to which this remoteness naturally gave rise (expressed in the clause, 'omne ignotum pro magnifico'), had hitherto saved them from attack. Now this remoteness had ceased to be (terminus Britanniae patet). Orelli takes 'famae' as a dative dependent on 'defendit.' Hitherto the remoteness of their abode (sinus) had saved them from fame, and they had been undisturbed because they had been unknown.

11. **Infestiores.**] Sc. more hostile than waves and rocks.

12. **Ambitiosi.**] Sc. eager for warlike glory. If the enemy has nothing to tempt their cupidity, they covet the glory of conquest for its own sake.

13. **Opes … concupiscunt.**] 'Wealth and poverty they covet with equal vehemence of desire,' sc. they spare neither the rich nor poor. Comp. for a similar sentiment, Sallust, *Cat.* 11, avaritia neque copia neque inopia minuitur.

14. **Ubi solitudinem faciunt.**] 'Where they make a solitude,' &c. &c.

CHAPTER XXXI.

1. **Alibi servituri.**] Sc. to serve elsewhere in the Roman armies. The degrading word 'servire' is of course deliberately chosen. It appears however that some at least of the British levies were retained in the island. See Ch. 18, auxiliarium quibus nota vada, and Ch. 32, agnoscent Britanni suam causam.

2. **Ager atque annus.**] This reading (due to Seyffert's emendation) is adopted by Ritter and Kritz, as coming closest to the Vatican MSS. which have 'aggerat annus,' and as yielding a good sense. 'Annus' is used in the *Germ.* Ch. 14, for the yearly

produce, which is here denoted by the somewhat rhetorical expression **ager atque annus**, just as bona fortunaeque expresses the simple notion of pecunia. By 'frumentum' is meant the corn exacted by the Romans. Comp. Ch. 19.

3. **Silvis ac paludibus emuniendis.**] 'In clearing woods and marshes.' Comp. the expression 'munitiones viarum,' *Ann.* 1. 56. The word 'emunire' implies throwing up causeways through morasses.

4. **Nata servituti.**] Comp. Sallust, *Jug.* 31, vos, Quirites, imperio *nati.*

5. **Semel veneunt.**] Boadicea is represented in Dio, LXII. 3 as saying, 'How much better would it be to be sold once for all than to be ransomed with the empty name of liberty from year to year.'

6. **Ultro...aluntur.**] Sc. slaves, so far from supplying their masters' maintenance (as we Britons have to do for the Romans) are supplied with what they want by their masters.

7. **Britannia...pascit.**] 'Britain is every day purchasing, every day supporting her own slavery.' She did the first by paying taxes, the second by supplying her masters with corn.

8. **Novi nos...petimur.**] 'We, as despicable new comers, are being marked out for destruction.' 'Novi' signifies 'new to slavery,' 'viles' those who are despicable because nothing is to be got out of them, as the next sentence implies.

9. **Neque enim arva nobis, &c.**] 'We have not, as the other Britons have, &c.' Calgacus is speaking only of Caledonia.

10. **Ferocia.**] 'High spirit.'

11. **Brigantes.**] In the account given, *Ann.* XIV. 31, of the British rising under Boadicea, the Trinobantes are mentioned, and the name of the Brigantes does not occur. It is possible that Calgacus here names them, as being one of the most powerful tribes, and closely bordering on Caledonia. All the MSS. have Brigantes. Ritter's substitution of Trinobantes seems purely arbitrary.

12. **Exurere coloniam.**] Sc. Camulodunum. Comp. Ch. 16, ipsam *coloniam* invasere ut sedem servitutis.

13. **Libertatem non in poenitentiam laturi.**] Sc. 'not about to bear our freedom so as to repent of it.' The meaning is, We do not intend, if successful, to sink into sloth (socordia) as the Brigantes did, and so to be subsequently conquered and reduced to a worse condition than that to which quiet submission

would have brought us—in which case we should have ultimately
cause for regret (poenitentia) that we had successfully resisted
for a while. It appears to us that the words as they stand will
fairly bear this interpretation, and that there is no need of Wex's
emendation, in libertatem *non* in poenitentiam arma laturi,
though, of course, it makes the passage somewhat easier, and
introduces the familiar phrase 'ferre arma.'

14. **Seposuerit.**] 'Has in reserve.' Comp. *Germ.* 29, in
usum praeliorum *sepositi.*

<h2 style="text-align:center">CHAPTER XXXII.</h2>

1. **Nisi.**] Orelli after the MSS. nisi si. But (as Wex
points out) where, as here, the word has an ironical force and
suggests an absurd alternative, it is never followed by si. 'Nisi
si ' would imply that the alternative was possible and reasonable.

2. **Commodent.**] The MSS. have commendent, for which
Puteolanus (whom nearly all modern editors follow) substituted
'commodent,' which precisely suits this passage. Comp. Livy,
XXXIV. 12, quamquam vereatur ne suas vires, aliis eas *commo-
dando,* minuat.

3. **Infirma vincla loco caritatis.**] Kritz reads 'loco'
from his own conjecture. The word seems to be wanted, as fear
and terror (metus ac terror) cannot well be said to be bonds of
affection. The meaning clearly is, that they take the place of it.

4. **Nulla plerisque patria.**] This would necessarily be
the case in an army made up of various nations whose separate
existence had been destroyed by conquest.

5. **Trepidos ignorantia.**] By 'ignorantia' is meant
specially ignorance of the country in which they were fighting.

6. **Circumspectantes.**] The notion of the word circum-
spectare is that of looking round timidly and suspiciously. This
is well illustrated in Cic. *Tusc.* I. 30, 73, Itaque *dubitans, cir-
cumspectans, haesitans,* multa adversa reverens, tamquam rate
in mari immenso nostra vehitur oratio.

7. **Vinctos.**] Comp. *Ann.* I. 62, eodem fato *vinctae* legiones, and *Hist.* I. 79, Sarmatae...velut *vincti* caedebantur.

8. **Nostras manus.**] Sc. troops who in heart are with us

9. **Agnoscent Britanni.**] Sc. Britons, compelled to fight
as levies in the Roman army.

10. **Senum coloniae.**] Comp. Ch. 5, incensae *coloniae.*

'Sories' in allusion to the 'veterans' by whom the coloniae were usually garrisoned.

11. **Aegra municipia.**] This is in apposition with 'senum coloniae.' The word 'aegra' denotes the feebleness arising from internal discord. Comp. its use *Hist.* II. 86, movere et quatere quidquid usquam *aegrum* foret, adgrediuntur. (The Greek νοσεῖν is used in precisely the same way. Soph. *El.* 1070, τὰ μὲν ἐκ δόμων νοσεῖ.) Comp. also Claudian, *Bell. Get.* 437, vivusque color redit urbibus *aegris.* Londinium and Verulamium had the character of 'municipia,' that is, they had their own 'senatus,' and their own officers for the administration of justice. 'Municipia' appears to us on the whole a better reading than that of 'mancipia' which Wex and Kritz adopt from the margin of one of the Vatican MSS., interpreting the words to mean 'a feeble and mutinous set of slaves.' This is hardly an appropriate description of the Roman 'veterani.'

12. **In hoc campo est.**] 'Rests with this battle-field.'

CHAPTER XXXIII.

1. **Alacres.**] With enthusiasm.

2. **Ut barbaris moris.**] Comp. 39, ut Domitiano *moris* erat.

3. **Armorum......procursu.**] 'There was the gleam of arms as every boldest soldier stepped to the front.'

4. **Instruebatur acies.**] Sc. the Caledonian army.

5. **Octavus annus.**] Agricola was now entering on his 8th year in Britain.

6. **Virtute et auspiciis imperii Romani.**] The 'auspicia' from the time of Augustus, properly speaking, belonged to the Emperor. Tacitus here affects the old republican form of speech. He may naturally have shrunk from any such allusion to Domitian, as the word imperatoris would have involved. When 'ductus' and 'auspicia' are used in close connexion, the first denotes the general's conduct of a campaign, the second the emperor's supreme direction and authority. So Suet. *Oct.* 21, domuit partim *ductu*, partim *auspiciis* suis Cantabriam, Aquitaniam, &c.

7. **Tot expeditionibus, &c.**] 'In the course of so many campaigns,' &c.

8. **Finem...tenemus.**] 'We are occupying the extremity of Britain not in mere report or rumour, but with an actual camp and armed force.'

9. **Inventa Britannia.]** Sc. Britain has been thoroughly discovered.

10. **Vota virtusque in aperto.]** 'Your wishes and your bravery have free scope.' Comp. Ch. 1, pronum magisque *in aperto.*

11. **Omniaque...adversa.]** Comp. Sall. *Cat.* 58, si vincimus, omnia nobis tuta erunt; sin metu cesserimus, eadem illa *adversa* fient.

12. **In frontem.]** Sc. for an advancing army. 'Frons' denotes here the presenting a face to the enemy, and thus implies progress.

13. **Terga.]** Sc. 'retreat.'

14. **Naturae fine.]** Comp. *Germ.* c. 45, illuc usque tantum *natura,* and see note on passage.

CHAPTER XXXIV.

1. **Vestra decora.]** The word 'decus' is here used in a less precise sense than that which it has Ch. 29, sua quisque *decora* gestantes. Here it means 'glorious deeds.' Livy, XXI. 43, uses it in just the same sense, Nemo vestrum est cui non idem ego virtutis spectator ac testis notata temporibus locisque referre sua possim *decora.*

2. **Unam legionem.]** Sc. the 9th legion. See Ch. 26.

3. **Furto noctis.]** Sc. an attack made under the cover of night. Curtius, IV. 13, uses the same expression, meae gloriae *furtum noctis* obstare non patiar.

4. **Clamore debellastis.]** 'You crushed with a mere shout.'

5. **Quomodo...pelluntur.]** We take this to be a general sentiment, which is the view of Orelli and Ritter. With the latter, we think it best to understand 'ruere' as equivalent to 'ruere solet,' and the following 'pelluntur' seems to favour this view. Similar instances of a sudden change of construction occur elsewhere. Comp. *Ann.* III. 26, postquam *exui* aequalitas et pro modestia et pudore ambitio et vis *incedebat*; and XII. 51, ubi *quati* uterus et viscera *vibrantur.* Curtius, III. 8, 19, has a very similar comparison: Delituisse inter angustias saltus ritu ignobilium ferarum quae strepitu praetereuntium audito silvarum latebris se occuluerunt.

6. **Numerus.]** The word is expressive of contempt, 'mere ciphers.' Comp. Hor. *Epist.* I. 2, 27, Nos *numerus* sumus et fruges consumere nati.

7. **Quos quod...restiterunt.**] 'That you have at last found them is not because they have stood their ground,' &c.

8. **Novissimae res...aciem.**] This is the reading of both the Vatican MSS. and, though harsh, is intelligible. 'Their desperate fortunes and their bodies in the extremity of panic have rivetted their line to this spot,' &c. Comp. for the use of 'novissimae' *Germ.* 24, extremo ac *novissimo* jactu. 'Defixere' vividly expresses the paralysis of terror. Kritz, in his 2nd edition, adopts the ingenious conjecture of Schoemann, novissimae res et extremius metus torpore defixere, &c.

9. **Victoriam ederetis.**] The expression 'edere victoriam' derives its meaning from the epithets attached to victoriam, and it conveys the notion of 'exhibiting on a grand scale.'

10. **Transigite cum expeditionibus.**] 'Make an end of campaigns.' 'Transigere' is a legal word, and denotes the settlement of a suit. Comp. *Germ.* 19, cum spe votoque uxoris *semel transigitur.*

11. **Imponite...diem.**] 'Crown fifty years' service with a great day.' Forty-two years, from A.D. 43 (the date of Claudius's expedition), was the precise period.

12. **Moras belli.**] Sc. carrying on war without energy, or wilfully protracting it. Comp. what is said of Vocula, *Hist.* IV. 34.

13. **Caussas rebellandi.**] This phrase would naturally mean the wrong doings of the dominant race. Comp. Ch. 19, doctus per aliena experimenta parum profici armis si injuriae sequerentur, *caussas* bellorum statuit excidere. But how was the army to shew upon a battle-field that it was guiltless of such practices? Perhaps we should understand by 'caussae' the pretexts or suggestions of possible rebellion which the carelessness of the conquerors might give, or which were the effective causes of rebellion. The soldiers were to do their work so thoroughly that there should be no strength left for rebellion.

CHAPTER XXXV.

1. **Affunderentur.**] This word (where we should have expected simply adderentur) seems intended to denote the rapid movements of cavalry.

2. **Ingens...bellandi.**] 'Bellandi,' the reading of the best MSS., must be construed with 'decus,' and 'victoriae' seems best taken as the dative. If the legions sustained no loss, this would add to the victory the great glory of fighting without shedding the blood of Roman soldiers.

3. **Si pellerentur.**] Sc. 'if the auxiliaries were repulsed.'

4. **In speciem ac terrorem.**] Sc. with a view to an imposing appearance and to cause panic. 'Species' is used in a similar way, Ch. 25, [classis]...sequebatur egregia *specie.*

5. **Connexi.**] The MSS. fluctuate between connexi and convexi. Connexi (the reading of Ritter and Kritz) implies that the line of the Britons extended without a break up the slope of the hill. Convexi, applied to this sloping formation, might be harsh, but Kritz surely goes too far in pronouncing it absurd. The word, however, does not seem to be much wanted.

6. **Media campi.**] Sc. the space between the two armies.

7. **Covinnarius eques.**] So the best MSS. and the most recent editors. The phrase must be simply equivalent to 'covinnarii,' which word occurs in the following chapter. The word 'covinnus,' according to Pomponius Mela (III. 6), denoted a chariot armed with scythes. The Britons, it seemed, borrowed it from the Belgae. Caesar, *B. G.* IV. 24 (where he describes this mode of fighting), says nothing about the chariots having scythes, nor does he use the words 'covinnus,' 'covinnarii.' He speaks of 'essedarii' (by which he meant the same thing), and he draws a distinction between them and regular cavalry (equitatus), which he says the Britons also employed. Tacitus makes no such direct allusion to cavalry; he merely tells us, Ch. 12, that some tribes fought with the chariot, among whom, it appears, were the Caledonians.

8. **Porrectior.**] 'Too extended.'

9. **Promptior in spem.**] Comp. *Ann.* xv. 25, *promptus* in pavorem. *Ib.* 61, *promptum* in adulationes ingenium.

10. **Firmus adversis.**] 'Resolute under adverse circumstances.'

11. **Ante vexilla.**] By 'vexilla' is meant the same as in Ch. 18, contractis legionum *vexillis*, where see note 13. Agricola took his stand in front of the peditum auxilia, mentioned above, among which would be several bodies of troops, termed vexilla.

CHAPTER XXXVI.

1. **Constantia.**] Sc. calm, self-possessed courage.

2. **Cetris.**] The 'cetra' was a small leathern shield, like the pelta. It appears from Livy XXXI. 36 that 'cetrati' and 'peltastae' were convertible terms.

3. **Batavorum cohortes.**] These are continually mentioned in the *Historiae*, and it appears that eight cohorts formed the 'auxilia' of the 14th legion. They were brave but turbulent troops.

4. **Quod.**] Sc. which mode of fighting.

5. **In aperto.**] The reading of the Vatican MSS. and, as it seems, quite defensible. The idea is that of hand-to-hand fighting in a free open space, where the best and most convenient weapons would be sure to tell. 'In arcto' (the reading adopted by Ritter and Kritz) is a purely arbitrary conjecture. Livy, XXXVIII. 41, thus describes a similar engagement: etsi iniquo loco, praelio tamen justo, acie *aperta*, collatis armis perquandum erat. The ground might be uneven; all that is meant is that it was clear of obstacles. Comp. the Greek military phrase ὕπαιθρος.

6. **Miscere ictus.**] Sc. to inflict blows at close quarters.

7. **Connisae.**] 'Straining every effort.' This is the reading of the best MSS. and is adopted by the recent editors.

8. **Interim...haerebant.**] This is a somewhat confused sentence, about the reading and punctuation of which editors vary. The question is whether the 'equitum turmae' were those of the Romans or the Britons. If the former, we must either read 'ut fugere' with Kritz, or take 'fugere covinnarii' with Ritter, as parenthetically introduced, which seems exceedingly awkward, and improbable. In this case 'equitum turmae' would no doubt be identical with the 3000 cavalry which, as appears from Ch. 35, were posted on the wings of the Roman army. The word 'turmae' (a technical military term) would certainly seem to point to a *Roman* rather than to any other force. It is, however, applied *Ann.* XIV. 34 to the Britons (Britannorum copiae passim per catervas et *turmas* exsultabant), and it must be remembered that Caesar expressly mentions cavalry among the various kinds of military force employed by them. It is thus possible that Orelli's view of the passage (we have followed his punctuation), taking 'equitum turmae' to mean the Caledonian cavalry, may be correct. It is not satisfactory, but other explanations seem to involve an alteration of the text or a very harsh interpretation. There can, we think, be no doubt that by 'hostium' in the succeeding clause is meant the Caledonians. The 'covinnarii' (though they produced a sudden panic) soon became entangled in the dense masses of their army's infantry, and were rendered useless by the unevenness of the ground.

9. **Minimeque...impellerentur.**] This is a corrupt passage which Orelli gives up. We have retained 'equestris' (as the Vatican MSS. have 'equestres'), and then follow Kritz in reading

aegre clivo instantes, which is not a violent departure from the MSS., and which certainly yields a satisfactory meaning. It was not like a regular cavalry engagement, as it was fought on sloping ground, on which they could barely keep their footing. On such ground too, the infantry would be peculiarly liable to be thrown down by the pressure of the cavalry horses which were drawn up among them. Wex's ingenious conjecture 'aequa nostris ea jam pugnae facies erat,' does not appear to be absolutely required.

10. **Transversos aut obvios.**] These words are, probably, to be referred to the Romans. Lipsius, however, understood them of the Britons.

CHAPTER XXXVII.

1. **Vacui.**] This means much the same as 'securi.' Here, as frequently, the less usual word is preferred by Tacitus.

2. **Ad subita belli.**] 'For the sudden emergencies of war.' The same phrase occurs *Hist.* v. 13.

3. **Ferocius.**] The word implies the notion of 'dash' and 'impetuosity.'

4. **In ipsos versum.**] 'Recoiled upon themselves.' The Britons who tried to take the Romans in rear, were themselves thus attacked.

5. **Aversam hostium aciem.**] Sc. 'the enemy's rear.'

6. **Tum vero, &c.**] Tacitus, as Lipsius was the first to point out, seems to have had in his mind the following passage from Sallust, *Jug.* 101 : tum spectaculum horribile campis patentibus; sequi, fugere, occidi capi, equi, viri afflicti; ac multi vulneribus acceptis neque fugere posse neque quietem pati, niti modo ac statim concidere; postremo omnia qua visus erat constrata telis, armis, cadaveribus, et inter ea humus infecta sanguine. With the words 'aliquando etiam victis ira virtus' may be compared Virg. *Aen.* II. 367, quondam etiam victis redit in praecordia virtus.

7. **Collecti...ignaros.**] This from the time of Puteolanus has been the common reading, and is adhered to by Orelli. It does not appear to have been satisfactorily emended by the efforts of recent editors. Something stands in the MSS. before 'collecti,' which Ritter conjectures to be inde, Halm (whom Kritz follows) more ingeniously, identidem, which conveys the idea of repeated sudden attacks made by the flying army on the pursuers. The general sense of the passage is clear enough, but we can hardly hope to restore the original with precision.

8. **Indaginis modo.**] 'Indago' denoted the process of enclosing a wood and stopping up all its outlets with nets, dogs, watchers, &c. Comp. Virg. *Aen.* IV. 121, Dum trepidant alae silvasque *indagine* cingunt. The 'validae et expeditae cohortes' were to surround the woods at all points and cut off the enemy's escape. Comp. Livy VII. 37, quum praemissus eques velut *indagine* dissipatos Samnites ageret. In *Ann.* XIII. 42, the word is used of the cunning arts of the fortune-hunters, Romae testamenta et orbos velut *indagine* ejus capi.

9. **Rariores silvas.**] 'The less dense parts of the forest.'

10. **Persultare.**] 'To scour.'

11. **In fugam versi.**] 'They turned to flight.'

12. **Vitabundi invicem.**] 'Avoiding one another.'

CHAPTER XXXVIII.

1. **Ultro incendere.**] 'Actually fired then.' 'Ultro' denotes the doing something altogether unexpected and unnecessary.

2. **Consilia aliqua.**] The addition of the word 'aliqua' is meant to imply that the Britons made only a few weak efforts at united action. 'They occasionally held counsel together.'

3. **Separare.**] Sc. 'consilia.' Instead of consulting together (miscere consilia), each thought only of his own safety.

4. **Pignorum.**] Sc. their wives and children. Comp. *Germ.* 7, in proximo *pignora* ('close at hand are those dearest to them').

5. **Concitari.**] 'Were roused to fury.'

6. **Tamquam misererentur.**] They were really urged to this act by rage; they pretended to be moved by pity for the lot of their wives and children.

7. **Vastum ubique silentium.**] 'Everywhere a gloomy silence.' Comp. *Ann.* III. 4, dies per *silentium vastus*. The notion of gloom and solitude is what the word 'vastus' specially and primarily denotes.

8. **Secreti colles.**] 'Deserted hills.' Comp. Virg. *Aen.* VI. 443, *secreti celant calles*.

9. **Spargi bellum.**] Comp. *Ann.* III. 21, Tacfarinas *spargit* bellum, sc. wages war at several points.

T. A.   6

10. **Borestorum.]** The name occurs nowhere else. The tribe of the Boresti must have dwelt to the north of Bodotria, possibly in Fife.

11. **Vires.]** 'A military force.'

12. **Secunda tempestate ac fama.]** 'With favourable weather and great renown.'

13. **Unde proximo...redierat.]** 'Unde' is to be construed with 'lecto,' not, as might seem at first sight, with 'redierat.' The meaning of this somewhat obscurely expressed clause is that the fleet started on its cruise from the 'Trutulensis portus,' to which it returned. By 'proximum Britanniae latus' must be meant the shores adjacent to Bodotria, that is, the east coast of Scotland. It seems clear that the 'Trutulensis portus' must have been some point at no great distance from Bodotria. The voyage here described has been alluded to Ch. 10. Without being a circumnavigation of Britain, it was enough to prove the country to be an island.

CHAPTER XXXIX.

1. **Auctum.]** The MSS. have 'actum,' which seems utterly indefensible, though one or two editors retain and endeavour to explain it. *Auctum* (the correction of Lipsius) is read by nearly all recent editors.

2. **Ut Domitiano moris erat.]** Comp. for similar construction *Germ.* 13, arma sumere non cuiquam *moris*, *Germ.* 21, abeunti si quid poposcerit, concedere *moris*, and ch. 33, ut barbaris *moris*.

3. **Fronte laetus, pectore anxius.]** 'With joy on his countenance, anxiety at his heart.'

4. **Falsum e Germania triumphum.]** Comp. Dio, LXVII. 4, and Suet. *Dom.* VI. The first tells us that Domitian marched with an army into Germany and returned without even the sight of an enemy. Suetonius speaks of sundry engagements (varia praelia) on the strength of which he celebrated a twofold triumph (duplicem triumphum) over the Chatti and Daci. Pliny in his Panegyric, Ch. 16, contrasts the genuine triumphs of Trajan's reign with the mimici currus and falsae simulacra victoriae of a former period. Comp. also *Germ.* Ch. 37, ingentes C. Caesaris minae in ludibrium versae, and see note 22.

5. **At nunc veram, &c.]** The infinitives in this and the following sentences depend on inerat conscientia.

6. **Studia fori.]** Sc. the eloquence of the bar.

7. **Civilium artium decus.]** By 'civiles artes' is meant knowledge of the law and the pursuit of politics. Comp. *Ann.*

III. 75, Capito Ateius...principem in civitate locum *studiis civilibus* adsecutus, and *Hist.* II. 5, where Mucianus is described in comparison with Vespasian as 'aptior sermone, dispositu provisuque civilium rerum peritus.'

8. **In silentium acta.**] Comp. Ch. 2 and 3. The expression denotes not merely 'driven into obscurity,' but actually 'silenced.'

9. **Occuparet.**] 'Forestall.' The word is used in its strictest meaning.

10. **Cetera.**] Sc. all other distinctions.

11. **Dissimulari.**] 'Disregarded.' As we say, 'he could shut his eyes to them.'

12. **Ducis...esse.**] Sc. 'the greatness of a good general was something specially imperial.'

13. **Secreto suo satiatus.**] It might be thought that the word 'secretum' points to the emperor's 'Albana arx,' mentioned Ch. 45. It seems best however to refer it to his dark and secret purposes, which for the present he was satisfied with brooding over. He was as yet in no hurry to execute them. Pliny thus speaks of Domitian, *Paneg.* 48: Non adire quisquam non alloqui audebat tenebras semper secretumque captantem, nec umquam ex solitudine sua prodeuntem nisi ut solitudinem faceret. Comp. Ch. 22, Ceterum ex iracundia, etc., where a contrast between the characters of Agricola and Domitian is suggested.

14. **Reponere odium.**] Sc. to treasure up his hatred. Recondere is used in a similar way, *Ann.* I. 69, Accendebat haec onerabatque Sejanus, peritia morum Tiberii odia in longum jaciens quae reconderet auctaque promeret. Comp. also *Ann.* XVI. 5, Adversus illustres dissimulatum ad praesens odium et mox redditum.

15. **Impetus famae.**] Sc. the first burst of his popularity.

CHAPTER XL.

1. **Triumphalia ornamenta.**] These comprised the 'corona laurea,' 'toga praetexta,' 'tunica palmata,' and 'sella curulis.' The 'statua illustris' (not necessarily included among these ornamenta) is elsewhere termed 'laureata,' and 'triumphalis.' See *Ann.* IV. 23, XV. 72, and *Hist.* I. 79.

2. **Quicquid pro triumpho datur.**] Sc. the 'supplicatio' (which usually preceded the triumph itself), and the 'sacra' con-

nected with it. As in Agricola's case, the ceremony of the sup-plicatio was not invariably followed by the grand triumphal pro-cession.

3. **Opinionem.**] 'A general impression.' The word has been wrongly understood of an impression produced in the mind of Agricola.

4. **Majoribus reservatam.**] 'Reserved for men of more than ordinary distinction.' Syria was a particularly rich pro-vince, and its government was the best post at the emperor's disposal.

5. **Sive ex ingenio...est.**] 'Or whether (the story) was invented and made up to suit the emperor's character.'

6. **Tradiderat.**] Agricola left Britain A.D. 85. We do not know who succeeded him. We are told by Suetonius (*Dom.* X.) of a Sallustius Lucullus, a governor of Britain, who was put to death by Domitian for allowing a new kind of lance to be called a Lucullea. It is just possible that this was Agricola's successor.

7. **Amicorum officio.**] Sc. the complimentary attentions of friends.

8. **Brevi osculo.**] Comp. *Ann.* XIII. 18, where Nero is said to have left his mother, 'post *breve osculum.*'

9. **Turbae servientium.**] 'The crowd of servile courtiers.'

10. **Grave inter otiosos.**] Sc. 'an object of dislike to men of leisure,' such as were the civilians about the emperor's court.

11. **Penitus auxit.**] Sc. he carried to the furthermost pos-sible limit. This must be the meaning of 'auxit,' if it is the right reading. Wex reads from his own conjecture 'hausit,' which seems a more appropriate word. The MSS. however all have 'auxit,' which may perhaps bear the meaning we have assigned to it.

12. **Cultu modicus.**] 'Cultus' denotes generally a man's external style of life, and would refer to his dress, house, furni-ture, establishment, &c. Comp. Plin. *Epp.* I. 22, quam parcus [Aristo] in victu, quam *modicus in cultu.*

13. **Quibus...mos est.**] 'Whose habit it is to judge of great men by external show.' 'Ambitio' specially signifies the kind of show and splendour which at Rome took the form of being waited on by a number of clients.

14. **Quaererent...... interpretarentur.**] 'Asked the reason of (Agricola's) fame, only a few could give the right answer.'

CHAPTER XLI.

1. **Laudantes.**] Comp. for a similar use of the participle Ch. 4, peccantium, Ch. 40, servientium.

2. **In Moesia Daciaque.** This refers to Domitian's war in Dacia, which was begun by the Dacian chief Decebalus A. D. 86. The Daci entered Moesia and stormed the winter-camp of the legions.

3. **In Germania et Pannonia.**] This appears from Dio, LXVII. 7, to be an allusion to losses sustained by Roman armies in the territories of the Marcomanni and Quadi.

4. **Militares viri.**] Wex, as it seems, without sufficient reason reads vici. The MSS. have viri, and the phrase 'vir militaris' is applied to Corbulo, *Ann.* xv. 26. Sallust too, *Cat.* 45, uses the similar expression 'homines militares.'

5. **Expugnati.**] A word rarely used of persons, but almost always of towns, fortresses, &c. We find however in Livy, XXIII. 30, nec ulla magis vis obsessos·quam fames *expugnavit.* A similar use of ἐκπολιορκεῖν (the Greek equivalent to expugnare) occurs in Thucyd. I. 134, τὸν Παυσανίαν ἐξεπολιόρκησαν λιμῷ.

6. **Limite imperii.**] 'Limes' denotes the actual fortified boundary line which had been drawn for the defence of the empire against the German and Sarmatian tribes on the side of Pannonia and Dacia.

7. **Ripa.**] Sc. the bank of the Danube, which for a considerable period had been in Roman hands, and was one of the great boundaries of the empire.

8. **Funeribus et cladibus.**] The first word may be meant to denote family losses, the second, those of the state. It is however quite possible that no such distinction is implied, and that the words are coupled together for the sake of rhetorical effect, as the general character of the passage would seem to suggest.

9. **Constantiam.**] 'Steady bravery.'

10. **Ceterorum.**] So Kritz after H. Grotius, whose emendation appears to be the best, though it must be admitted that the rhythm of the sentence rather halts. The Vatican MSS. have eorum, after which something appears to have dropped out.

11. **Verberatas.**] A strong word, used to imply that a deep impression was made on the emperor.

12. **Principem exstimulabant.**] 'Were working powerfully on the emperor's feelings.' This is one of the rare instances of the use of dum with the imperfect indicative.

13. **Vitiis aliorum.**] 'Vitium' here includes faults of incapacity (which have been hinted at in the words inertia et formidine ceterorum) and the moral faults above named of 'malignitas' and 'livor.'

14. **In ipsam......agebatur.**] 'Praeceps agi' expresses the notion of being hurried to ruin. In Agricola's case the glory (which was, as it were, thrust upon him) was his ruin. Two thoughts are combined in the sentence, (1) Agricola's rapid rise to greatness, (2) the fatal dangers of that greatness. 'In ipsam gloriam,' 'to the very height of glory.'

CHAPTER XLII.

1. **Aderat jam annus.**] Probably the 5th year after Agricola's return from Britain, or A. D. 90. By this time he would be among the oldest of the consulars, and as such might look for either of the provinces here named.

2. **Asiae et Africae.**] Sc. the proconsulate of either Asia or Africa. Both were senatorian provinces.

3. **Civica.**] Comp. Suetonius (*Dom.* x.) where we are told that among other senators of consular rank put to death by Domitian was Civica Cerialis, who was at the time proconsul of Asia. This gives force to the words 'nec Domitiano exemplum.'

4. **Consilium.**] Sc. the means of knowing how to act.

5. **Exemplum.**] 'A precedent.'

6. **Cogitationum principis periti.**] 'Familiar with the emperor's views.'

7. **Ultro Agricolam interrogarent.**] 'Went so far as to ask Agricola.'

8. **Occultius.**] 'In somewhat obscure hints.'

9. **Mox......offerre.**] Soon after they offered their services in making good his excuse, sc. in satisfying the emperor's mind as to Agricola's reasons for declining a province.

10. **Non jam obscuri.**] 'No longer hiding their purpose;' throwing off the mask.

11. **Pertraxere.**] 'Brought him against his will.'

12. **Paratus simulatione.**] This has been understood to

mean 'having a stock of hypocrisy always ready ;' 'completely
furnished with it.' It is better, we think, to take the words as
if they meant 'armed with hypocrisy.' This seems more vigorous and Tacitean.

13. **In arrogantiam compositus.**] 'Assuming a haughty
demeanour.' The emperor affected complete indifference to the
matter.

14. **Agi sibi gratias passus est.**] Seneca (*de Tranq.*
14) mentions a yet stronger instance of the encouragement of
servility in Caligula, who allowed those whose children he had
put to death, and those whose property he had confiscated, form-
ally to thank him.

15. **Beneficii invidia.**] 'The invidious character of the
favour.' The favour granted to Agricola was such as would
bring odium (invidia) on the emperor with all right-thinking men.

16. **Salarium.**] According to Dio, LII. 23, it was Mae-
cenas who advised Augustus that salaries should be paid to the
governors of provinces. The same writer tells us (LXXVIII. 22),
that under the emperor Macrinus (A. D. 218), Aufidius Fronto
who was to have been proconsul of Africa or Asia, but who did
not go to either province, received the sum of 1,000,000 sesterces,
or about £8000, and he implies that this was the regular scale
of payment.

17. **Sive ex conscientia.**] 'Or from a bad conscience.'
This is substantially the meaning of 'conscientia,' though here and
elsewhere it differs slightly from its derivative, 'conscience,' and
answers more exactly to 'consciousness.' Here it implies 'consciousness of hypocrisy or double-dealing.'

18. **Ne...emisse.**] 'Fearing that he might be thought to
have gained by a bribe what he had forbidden.' The emperor was
afraid people would say that he had not the strength or courage
to forbid Agricola from going to his province, but had been
obliged to bribe him with the salarium.

19. **Quo obscurior eo irrevocabilior.**] 'Implacable in
proportion to its reserve.'

20. **Prudentia.**] 'Good sense.'

21. **Inani jactatione libertatis.**] 'By a useless parade of
freedom.'

22. **Quibus......mirari.**] 'Those who make a point of ad-
miring lawless behaviour.' 'Ilicitus' denotes not merely what is
contrary to good manners, but what is actually forbidden by law.
Here therefore it would imply 'conduct in defiance of the emperor's

authority.' Possibly in this sentence and in the words 'inani jactatione' there is an indirect allusion to some of the extreme affections of Stoicism.

23. **Modestiam.]** 'Quiet, orderly demeanour.' Along with this the idea of self-control is implied.

24. **Eo laudis excedere.]** 'Rise to that degree of distinction.' 'Excedere' denotes the transcending ordinary limits. Lipsius needlessly conjectured 'escendere.'

25. **Per abrupta.]** 'By steep (and, consequently, danger-ous) paths.' The meaning of the phrase is explained and illustrated by a passage in *Ann.* IV. 20, an licent inter *abruptam* contumaciam et deforme obsequium pergere iter ambitione ac periculis vacuum. The notion of 'abrupta contumacia,' as here of per abrupta, is a defiant disregard of all that custom and public opinion sanction and require. *ifagd nip*

26. **Ambitiosa morte inclaruerunt.]** 'Have become famous by a death intended for effect.' Ambitiosus, 'desirous to win applause;' ambitiosae preces (*Hist.* II. 49), 'prayers very anxious to gain their end,' hence 'importunate.' Comp. Ch. 29, quem casum neque ambitiose......tulit, and see note 2.

CHAPTER XLIII.

1. **Finis vitae, &c. &c.]** Comp. this and the following chapters with Cicero's remarks on the death of Lucius Crassus (Cic. *De Orat.* III. 2, 3), a passage which Tacitus would seem to have had in his mind.

2. **Extraneis.]** Sc. Those who were neither relatives nor intimate friends. The death of Germanicus excited similar grief. See *Ann.* III. 1, 2, where it is said 'idem omnium gemitus; neque discerneres proximos alienos.'

3. **Vulgus et hic aliud agens populus.]** No marked distinction is intended between *vulgus* and *populus.* Both words denote the lowest and poorest class, as in *Dialog.* 7, *vulgus* imperitum et tunicatus hic *populus* (*tunicatus* meaning those who were too poor to wear the 'toga,' comp. Hor. *Epp.* I. 7, 65, *tunicato* popello) and as in *Hist.* I. 89, *vulgus* et magnitudine nimia communium curarum expers *populus.* Comp. also *Hist.* II. 90, *vulgus* vacuum curis. These passages explain and illustrate the meaning of '*aliud agens*' which implies inattention and indifference to public events, and is thus almost equivalent to 'incuriosus.' The phrase 'alias res agere' means "to be inattentive to the matter in hand." See Ter. *Eun.* II. 3, 57, *alias res agis*;

Cic. *Brutus*, 66, 233, omnia magna voce dicens, verborum sane bonorum cursu incitato, ita furebat tamen ut mirarere tam *alias res agere* populum ut esset insano inter disertos locus. Comp. also Pliny, *Paneg.* 5 tibi (sc. Trajano) *quanquam non id agentium,* civium clamor occurrit.

4. **Fora.**] Sc. what the French call les places publiques.

5. **Circulos.**] Sc. little knots or gatherings for gossip.

6. **Locuti sunt.**] 'Talked of him.' Understand 'eum.' Comp. *Ann.* XVI. 22, te, Nero, et Thraseam civitas *loquitur.*

7. **Constans rumor.**] Sc. a generally current and uncontradicted report. Dio, LXVI. 20, positively asserts its truth. Suetonius however does not include Agricola in the number of senators and men of consular rank put to death by Domitian (Suet. *Domit.* 10).

8. **Nobis nihil comperti affirmare ausim.**] 'I would venture to affirm that we have no certain knowledge.' We have followed the reading of the MSS. according to which 'esse' must be understood after 'comperti.' If this reading is correct, Tacitus appears to mean that all he can state positively is that to himself the whole affair was wrapped in obscurity. In the two following sentences he insinuates the worst; in this, he leaves it an open question, on which others may make up their minds, if they can. Ritter and Wex emend the passage; the first inserts *ut,* the second *quodve,* after 'comperti.' As it stands, it is certainly somewhat obscure. There is however no real difficulty about the sudden change from the plural to the singular in 'nobis, ausim.' Instances of this are by no means rare. Comp. *Ann.* XIV. 43, simul quidquid hoc in *nobis* auctoritatis est, crebris contradictionibus destruendum non *existimabam.*

9. **Principatus.**] Sc. the imperial court.

10. **Medicorum intimi.**] Comp. *Ann.* IV. 3, where in the account of Sejanus's plot against the life of Drusus, Livia, the wife of the latter, is said to have made a 'confidant' of one Eudemus, a physician (sumitur in conscientiam Eudemus, amicus ac medicus Liviae, specie artis frequens secretis).

11. **Inquisitio.**] 'Espionage.'

12. **Momenta ipsa deficientis.**] 'Momentum' answers to ῥοπή and denotes (1) the turn of the scale, (2) the critical moment at which the turn takes place. Hence here it signifies all the various symptoms of approaching death.

13. **Per dispositos cursores.**] Sc. messengers between Rome and Domitian's 'villa Albana,' on which see ch. 45.

14. **Animo vultuque.**] It is not necessary to explain this as a hendiadis. 'Animus' denotes the frame of mind which inclines a person to the usual manifestations of grief, 'vultus,' its expression in the countenance. Domitian's assumed grief, showed itself not merely in his looks but in his general demeanour.

15. **Securus jam odii.**] 'Being now careless of his hatred.' Domitian was now free from the anxiety with which his hatred of Agricola had filled him. Consequently, being at ease in his mind, he could, in spite of his natural irascibility, so far control himself as to exhibit a show of sorrow. This he could not do as long as he was afraid.

16. **Coheredem.**] This probably implies that Agricola made the emperor heir to *half* his estate.

17. **Piissimae.**] A form disapproved by writers of the Augustan age. Cicero (*Philip.* XIII. 19) twits M. Antonius with having used it in reference to Lepidus.

18. **Velut honore judicioque.**] '(he was greatly pleased) as if it were a compliment and a free choice.' Domitian in this instance followed the example of such emperors as Caligula and Nero, to the latter of whom Prasutagus, king of the Iceni, and husband of Boadicea, paid the same compliment with the same hope as Agricola, See *Ann.* XIV. 31. Comp. also *Ann.* XVI. 11, where L. Vetus, one of Nero's victims, is advised *magna ex parte Caesarem haeredem nuncupare*, atque ita nepotibus de reliquo consulere. Domitian, who at first refused to receive any legacies from those who had children, would afterwards claim a deceased person's estate on the slightest evidence. See Suet. *Dom.* 9, 12. Pliny (*Paneg.* 43) speaks of the 'security of our wills' as one of the happy features of Trajan's reign. For 'judicio' comp. Suet. *Octav.* 66, where it is said of Augustus, that, though he refused to accept any legacy from strangers, amicorum tamen *suprema judicia* morosissime pensitavit.

CHAPTER XLIV.

1. **Decentior.**] 'Decens' denotes grace and symmetry of figure. The French translator Louandre thus renders the passage ; Sa taille était bien proportionnée sans être haute.

2. **Nihil metus in vultu.**] So Orelli and Wex. The MSS. vary. One has nihil metus et impetus, which can hardly be the true reading, though Kritz adopts it. 'Metus' here, as elsewhere, denotes that which causes fear. Comp. Quintil. *Instit.* VI. 2, 21 metum duplicem intelligi volo, *quem patimur*, et *quem facimus*. Possibly a contrast may be intended between Agricola and Domitian whom Pliny (*Paneg.* 48) describes as 'visu terribilis.'

3. **Gratia oris supererat.**] 'A gracious expression predominated' (*C* and *B*). 'Superesse' has a similar meaning ch. 45, omnia......*superfuere* honori tuo. Comp. also Germ. 6, ne ferrum quidem *superest,* and 26, *superest* ager.

4. **Integrae aetatis.**] A phrase answering to our expression "the prime of life."

5. **Quantum ad gloriam.**] 'As regards glory.' Comp. Germ. ch. 21, *quantum ad* jus hospitis.

6. **Impleverat.**] 'He had fully attained.' Comp. *Ann.* XIV. 54, uterque mensuram *implevimus,* and Plin. *Epp.* II. 1, 2, perfunctus est tertio consulatu ut summum fastigium privati hominis *impleret.*

7. **Triumphalibus ornamentis.**] See ch. 40, note 1.

8. **Opibus nimiis non gaudebat.**] 'Excessive wealth he did not possess.' Kritz' interpretation; 'he did not set a value on,' &c.

9. **Speciosae.**] Sc. sufficient wealth to make a handsome appearance.

10. **Filia...superstitibus.**] Wex reads filiae, uxori and connects them with the preceding 'speciosae contigerant.' His reason for so doing, that Agricola could not be pronounced happy because his daughter and wife survived him and were thus destined to see the evil days which he escaped, seems far-fetched. It must have been at least a comfort to him, as pointed out in the next chapter, to have had his wife by his side during his last illness.

11. **Nam sicuti...ominabatur.**] Ritter's emendation of this passage (which he accomplishes by substituting quondam for quod) appears to be the simplest, and we have (with Kritz) adopted it. We think too Kritz is right in reading hanc lucem for hac luce, as this is the regular construction with durare. There is, it must be admitted, considerable difficulty about the expression 'durare ominabatur,' which may however be compared with a passage in *Hist.* I. 50, erant qui Vespasianum et arma Orientis *augurarentur.* It may too be justified by the fact that sperare, a similar word, is occasionally construed with the *present* infinitive. According to Dio, LXIX. 12 (and Plin. *Paneg.* 5, 94), Trajan's elevation was foretold two years before Agricola's death, and to this Tacitus perhaps refers in 'augurio.' Or we may render 'Trajanum' by our expression 'a Trajan.' 'Augurio votisque ominabatur' is equivalent to 'augurabatur et vehementer optabat.'

12. **Grande solatium tulit.**] 'Solatium ferre' may be a similar expression to 'palmam ferre' (where ferre is for referre), in which case 'solatium' must be rendered by 'compensation.' Or (as Wex takes it) it may mean, 'he brought us great consolation for his premature death,' &c. &c.

13. **Spiramenta].** Sc. 'pauses.'

14. **Uno ictu.**] So Caligula was said to have wished that the Roman people had one neck, that he might have destroyed them at a blow. Comp. Senec. *de Ira,* III. 19.

15. **Rem publicam exhausit.**] 'Drained the life-blood of the state :' or 'exhausit' may be used as 'hausisse' in *Hist.* I. 41, 'to inflict a deadly wound,' jugulum ejus *hausisse.*

<h3 style="text-align:center">CHAPTER XLV.</h3>

1. **Non vidit etc.**] There is a marked resemblance between this passage and Cic. *de Orat.* III. 2, Non vidit (L. Crassus) flagrantem bello Italiam, non ardentem invidia senatum, non sceleris nefarii principes civitatis reos.

2. **Obsessam...senatum.**] These words point to some *one* occurrence, of which we know nothing from any other source. It appears from *Ann.* XVI. 27, that Nero intimidated the senate in a similar fashion.

3. **Consularium caedes.**] Suetonius (*Domit.* x.) gives a list of these murders, with the frivolous causes which provoked them. Among them were Civica Cerialis, proconsul of Asia ; Sallustius Lucullus, governor of Britain ; Salvius Cocceianus, nephew of the Emperor Otho ; Junius Rusticus ; the younger Helvidius, &c. &c.

4. **Nobilissimarum feminarum.**] Among these were Gratilla, the wife of Arulenus Rusticus ; Arria, the wife of Thrasea ; Faunia, his daughter, who twice accompanied her husband into exile, and was a third time banished on his account. See Plin. *Epp.* III. 11, VII. 19.

5. **Una adhuc victoria censebatur.**] 'As yet (at the time of Agricola's death) by one and only one victory was Carus Metius distinguished.' 'Censeri' is equivalent to 'aestimari,' and its precise meaning is that Metius's power for mischief was as yet estimated by but one successful information. It is thus used *Dial.* 39. ejusmodi libri extant ut ipsi quoque qui egerunt non aliis magis orationibus *censeantur,* and Plin. *Paneg.* 15, quisquis paullo vetustior miles, hic te commilitone *censetur.* The name of the notorious 'delator' Caius Metius meets us Plin. *Epp.* VII. 19, 5, VII. 27, 14, Juv. L 35, Mart. XII. 25. 5.

6. **Albanam arcem.**] This was one of Domitian's country seats. It was under the Alban Mount, and was 17 miles from

Rome. Tacitus, as also Juvenal, IV. 145, terms it 'arx,' to imply that it was a kind of centre and stronghold of imperial tyranny. Dio, LXVII. 1, describes it as the emperor's ἀκρόπολις. It was here that he convoked the 'pontifices' to pass sentence of death on the Vestal, Cornelia. See Plin. *Epp.* IV. 11. Not till the emperor's later years were the counsels (sententia) of Messalinus (whom Juvenal, IV. 115, describes as Grande et conspicuum nostro quoque tempore monstrum) heard beyond its walls.

7. **Massa Baebius.**] See *Hist.* IV. 50, and Plin. *Ep.* III. 4, VI. 29, VII. 33. He was impeached by the province of Baetica where he had been procurator.

8. **Nostrae...manus.**] Sc. the hands of us senators, of whom Tacitus at this time was one.

9. **Nos Maurici Rusticique, &c. &c.**] Wex, to avoid the somewhat bold zeugma in the passage as it stands, reads from the margin of one of the Vatican MSS. Nos Mauricum Rusticumque *divisimus.* This is a mere conjecture. Understand after 'visus' some such word as 'perculit' or 'afflixit.' The zeugma seems not too harsh for Tacitus.

10. **Quum suspiria nostra subscriberentur.**] 'When our sighs were made matter of accusation.' *Subscribere* (properly 'to sign one's name under that of the plaintiff or accuser') is continually used by the best writers as equivalent to 'accusare,' and 'indices' or 'accusatores' are also termed '*subscriptores.*' Quintilian, XII. 8. 8, has the expression *subscribere* audita (to make what has been heard the subject of a charge).

11. **Denotandis tot hominibus palloribus.**] Comp. *Ann.* III. 53, In hac relatione subtrahi oculos meos melius fuit, ne *denotantibus* vobis ora ac metum singulorum ipse etiam viderem eos ac velut deprehenderem. Denotare pallores is to mark out with a view to destruction the men whose faces are beginning to turn pale ; and the word 'denotare' answers to 'designare,' which is used in a similar way in Cic. *Cat.* I. 1. 2, notat et *designat* oculis ad caedem unumquemque nostrum. It seems clear that 'denotare' may be thus understood, and therefore Wex's conjecture, denotandis...*pallore oribus* (which, though probably Latin, strikes us as awkward) is needless. With this passage may be aptly compared Juvenal's description of Domitian's senate (IV. 74), proceres, In quorum facie miserae magnaeque sedebat Pallor amicitiae.

12. **Rubor...muniebat.**] The natural redness of Domitian's countenance (of which Pliny, *Paneg.* 48, and Suetonius, Domit. 18, both speak) rendered him proof against the ordinary manifestation of the feeling of shame. Comp. also *Hist.* IV. 40, *crebra oris confusio* pro modestia accipiebatur.

13. **Tu vero...mortis.]** So Cic. *de Orat.* III. 3. Ego vero, te, Crasse, quum vitae flore, tum *mortis opportunitate* divino consilio et ortum et exstinctum esse arbitror.

14. **Constans et libens.]** 'With courage and cheerfulness.'

15. **Tamquam...donares.]** 'As though to the best of thy power thou wert bestowing freedom from guilt on the emperor.' The phrase 'pro virili portione' ('parte' and not 'portione' is the word used by writers of the Augustan age) occurs *Hist.* III. 20, and denotes 'all that a man can do singly.' The expression 'innocentiam donares' seems intended to suggest that the emperor was not really innocent of Agricola's death.

16. **Longae absentiae condicione.]** 'By the necessity of a long absence.' Tacitus is speaking of *his own* absence from Rome.

17. **Paucioribus lacrimis.]** Sc. 'with too few tears.'

18. **Compositus.]** The reading of the MSS. is 'comploratus.' '*Compositus*, however, is found in the margin of one of the Vatican MSS., and is read by all recent editors except Kritz. It seems a far more suitable word than 'comploratus,' which savours too much of the noisy lamentations which in the next chapter Tacitus deprecates. Comp. *Hist.* I. 47, Pisonem Verania uxor et frater...*composuere*, and Hor. *Sat.* I. 9, 28, omnes composui.

19. **Desideravere aliquid.]** 'Longed for something in vain.'

CHAPTER XLVI.

1. **Ut sapientibus placet.]** 'As is believed by philosophers.'

2. **Infirmo desiderio.]** 'Feeble regret,' 'infirmus' denoting what belongs to a morbid state of mind.

3. **Lugeri...plangi.]** The *first* word expresses the sentiment of grief, the *second* its outward manifestations.

4. **Quam temporalibus laudibus.]** 'Quam' is due to Ursinus, and is certainly required if 'temporalibus' (which is the reading of the MSS.) be retained. The notion of *temporales laudes* (transitory praises) is the 'laudatio funebris,' which would be soon forgotten. This, we believe, is what Tacitus had in his mind. He himself, as Pliny (*Epp.* II. 1. 6) tells us, pronounced a funeral *éloge* over Verginius Rufus. Lipsius (whom Ritter follows) substituted from conjecture 'immortalibus' for temporalibus; but it would hardly have been in good taste for Tacitus to apply such an epithet to the present work.

5. **Si natura suppeditet.**] Sc. if our natural powers are equal to the task.

6. **Decoremus.**] 'Let us honour.' Comp. Ennius quoted by Cicero (*Tusc.* I. 15, 34), Nemo me lacrimis *decoret* nec funera fletu Faxit.

7. **Formamque ac figuram.**] *Formam* is the correction of Muretus for *famam*, the reading of the MSS., and is accepted by nearly all editors. Comp. Cic. *Tusc.* I. 16, 37, animorum *formam* aliquam atque *figuram* quaerebant. Tacitus uses the phrase to denote the whole mind and character of Agricola. Pliny also uses it in connection with a very similar sentiment (*Paneg.* 55), *formam* principis *figuramque* non aurum melius vel argentum quam favor hominum exprimat teneatque.

8. **Non quia...putem.**] 'Not because I think a veto ought to be put on,' &c. 'Intercedere' is strictly said of the *tribunitian* veto. The *subjunctive* implies, 'I am not one to think,' &c.

9. **Forma mentis.**] 'Mens' here = animus, and stands for the entire mental and spiritual being.

10. **Tenere et exprimere.**] 'Retain and represent.'

11. **Alienam materiam et artem.**] Sc. marble or bronze, and the art of sculpture, which are necessarily foreign (*alienus*) to the truest and best representation of human character.

12. **In aeternitate temporum.**] 'In the eternal succession of the ages.' (*C* and *B.*)

13. **Fama rerum.**] In the records of history, or more generally, 'the fame that waits on noble deeds.' (*C* and *B.*)

14. **Obruit.** This is Haupt's emendation for obruet, the reading of the MSS. It has the merit of bringing out more forcibly the antithesis between 'oblivio' and the words 'narratus et traditus.' The allusion in 'multos veterum' is to the times of the republic, and the general sentiment may be compared with the well-known passage in Horace, *C.* IV. 9. 25, Vixere fortes ante Agamemnona Multi; sed omnes illacrimabiles Urguentur ignotique longa Nocte, carent quia vate sacro. Tacitus thus hints more delicately at the effect of his work than he would do by describing it as 'laudes immortales.'

INDEX OF PROPER NAMES

INDEX OF WORDS AND PHRASES

EXPLAINED IN THE NOTES TO THE AGRICOLA.

The first Numeral refers to the Chapter, the second to the Note.

A.

A.

CAMBRIDGE: PRINTED BY C. J. CLAY & SONS, AT THE UNIVERSITY PRESS.